Before They Were Champs

A Boston Red Sox Story

GERARD PURCIELLO

PublishAmerica
Baltimore

© 2011 by Gerard Purciello.
All rights reserved. No part of this book may be reproduced, stored in a retrieval system or transmitted in any form or by any means without the prior written permission of the publishers, except by a reviewer who may quote brief passages in a review to be printed in a newspaper, magazine or journal.

First printing

All characters in this book are fictitious, and any resemblance to real persons, living or dead, is coincidental.

PublishAmerica has allowed this work to remain exactly as the author intended, verbatim, without editorial input.

Hardcover 978-1-4560-2882-4
Softcover 978-1-4560-2881-7
PUBLISHED BY PUBLISHAMERICA, LLLP
www.publishamerica.com
Baltimore

Printed in the United States of America

DEDICATION

For my Mom and Dad, brothers and sisters, all still very young at heart—my love. And to the characters who made this book possible. Thanks, you know who you are. We did it again, Uncle Vin!

ACKNOWLEDGEMENTS

A very special thank you to my niece Elena May whose artistic talents grace my book cover. Bravo principessa!
Contact Elena: design@elenamay.com

And to my nephew Danny Nyman, the pro behind the camera.

PROLOGUE

We ran hard and as long as our legs and lungs could take us, bumping and grabbing each other through the grass with only our flashlights to lead the way—there was no way I was going to allow them to get there first. I stumbled once, tripped almost, and nearly fell. I grabbed Capisce's arm to right myself and lunged—I was the first to reach our tent. I blurted out triumphantly with burning lungs, "we're…safe now…here…we…made it," as if a vinyl tent would protect us from the evils of the night bearing down on us. We tore through the opening of our impenetrable fortress and zipped us in and "them" out. Twotails hissed and jumped back not expecting our forced entry. We collapsed, breathing heavily but attempting to be quiet so as not to give away our secure place.

"Shut off the flashlights," I huffed, wiping blood off my face.

"Yeah, yeah," whispered Paulie.

"Hurry," croaked Capisce.

We sat in silence catching our breath. I slowly clicked on my flashlight and pointed the beam of light at Paulie, then Capisce, then back in Paulie's eyes. "Where's your brother?"

"My brother?"

"Yeah, your brother. Where's Lights?"

"I thought he was with you, I mean, in front of you."

"Don't look at me," added Capisce. "I thought he was in front of you."

I shut the flashlight off, afraid to move or speak. I could feel their eyes on me asking, "whatta we do now?"

We had lost Lights in the middle of the Vermont woods… with forest beasts breathing down his neck.

ONE

The summer nights were in full force, which normally would bring nothing but happiness and cheer into the lives of four eleven-year-olds. It meant no school, no rules (within certain rules), no homework, no real "early to bed" curfew, and no dress code. The summer carried so many non "no's" almost all of the fun of being a trouble-making kid was taken out of the whole process. What the summer nights carried like Santa's little gifts were the golden offerings that were meant for kids like us—Paul "Paulie" Beacon and twin brother Joe "Lights" Beacon, Peter "Capisce" Capiscio and me, Jerry "Tags" Taglia. The nights carried backyard sleep outs, connecting the stars, endless arguments on who was the best baseball player *ever*, and what video star bombshell we all wanted to hangout with. But all of these dwarfed in comparison to the sweetest sound carried across the warm summer evening air; the comforting voices of the radio announcers of the Boston Red Sox. We'd stare at the radio as if we were witnessing something deeply religious as the baseball announcer would remind us just how lucky we were to be only kids, and to be in the summer free no "no"zone. Cicada's songs were silenced. The bug zapper on Mr. Sal's back porch just a distant whimper. Even the volume from old man Pop Weisel's television from across the street was a minor distraction.

"*Waaaaay* back," mimicked Capisce.

"There's a drive," I echoed.

"Tell it soooo long everybodddddy," added Lights.

"Can *you* believe it?" said Paulie.

"Knockout," we all added as one, passing around lazy high-fives as we lay sprawled in my backyard. I pointed to the sky wearing my number "35" official Hilberto Otto white (I owned a red one, too) Red Sox jersey just like the star Red Sox left fielder did every time he hit a homer. He had just connected on a three-run home run, and on most nights we'd be slamming high-fives, but tonight the Otto blast did nothing but cut into a 10-0 Toronto lead. It was the bottom of the ninth and even *we,* the small part of the Boston Nation of Diehards, realized this one might have slipped away. The season was becoming desperate, and the summer was becoming an inside out reverse knockout—a stink bomb.

"What are we going to do?" asked Paulie, rubbing his hands on his matching official white Hilberto Otto jersey. Paulie and I played as a team today so we wore the matching Otto jerseys, Capisce and Lights wore their red number "18" Lefty Van Weller jerseys.

"What are *we* gonna do?" asked Capisce of Paulie.

"We gotta do somethin', right Tags?" Lights pleaded.

Yeah, right, I thought looking at their worried faces. I…we, couldn't believe it was happening again. Our favorite baseball team in the entire universe, our only team, was taking us on one of their usual roller-coaster rides of mental anguish.

"You remember last year, Tags? The Sox had that five game lead in September until the second to last week of the year and then blew it..." Paulie grumbled.

"Of course I remember."

"What about two years ago? They made it to the American League Championship Series, up two games to none over the..." Capisce put two fingers in his mouth and faked gaging, "the Jan-kees, only to looooose the series in seven."

"I know, I know, I remember." I was getting a popsicle headache.

"You remember when we were six and the team ended up in *last* place? Last place, I can't take *that* again. It's been, what, sixteen years since they last won the Series?"

"2007, Lights."

"Yeah, 2007. That's a long, long time. Sixteen years," mumbled Lights. "I don't want to die without seeing the Red Sox win a World Series."

"Tags, we can't sit around and do nuthin', can we?"

I glanced at Paulie, Lights and Capisce, and slowly shook my head. How many times in my life have I seen this? Every one of my eleven years, that's how many. I was tired of losing, my friends were tired of losing, everybody born after 2007... heck, one year after they had won it all Boston fans were tired of losing. As far as I knew no one was doing anything about it. Maybe the time was at hand *to do* something about it. But what, I thought, could four dopey kids from Belmont possibly do to help the Boston Red Sox win their first championship in...*in a very long time?* Something was better than nothing.

"Geez, it must've been something awesome to live back when the Red Sox were winning World Series. My dad told me that kids got to skip school and go to something called a rolling rally on boats."

"I want to go on a rolling rally on boats."

"I just want the Red Sox to win a championship before I get too old and don't care anymore."

"What is a rolling rally?"

"A parade…or somethin.'"

I listened to Mr. Sal's bug zapper. "That's seventy."

"Seventy what?" yawned Capisce.

As professional eleven year olds we could manage to change directions on our thoughts like our prized all-star pitcher Lefty Van Weller could on his curveball.

"No way, that's sixty-seven. Look, I marked every one." Lights held up his bug scorecard, a piece of paper with drawn mosquito's on them that I had done on my computer. For every zap you heard you'd make an "X" through the bug. I limited the number of bugs to seventy, mostly for time considerations (well, maybe for our short attention span, or lack-there-of). When your scorecard was full the one with the lowest number of "zaps" would have to buy the other three sodas the next day.

"Oh jeez, I forgot," said Capisce.

"I got sixty-three."

"Can't be seventy already. I only have sixty…one…two. I have sixty-two."

"Loooooser," laughed Paulie.

"Major loooser," snorted Lights.

Now, you don't want to be calling Capisce any names on account he could hurt you in a big way without really wanting to because he was as large as a house…a really, really BIG house. He weighed one-hundred pounds more than the twins and me, and his square face and black eyes reminded me of a black bear. When he lost his usual calm manner he *became* a black bear. I was praying this wasn't one of his moments.

I looked over at the twins as if to say, "are you out of your minds," and realized they must've felt the same because they were both getting to their feet to get out of town. Capisce, lying on his back, reached over his head and grabbed both of the guys by an ankle. It was a very impressive move, one I think that saved the twins an "atomic twister," which was almost worse than death itself. Capisce's twisters were Hall-of-Fame caliber. The method was simple, it was the wrist strength that separated the rookie from the professional. The ideal location was the fleshy part on the back of the arm or the back of the leg. If you'd ever had an atomic twister you know the pain is equal to a thousand bee stings. You grab the skin between the first finger and middle finger and you twist like you're turning a door knob. If the twister is, say, a grand-slam twister, the red welt stays on you for a solid four days.

"Whoa, nice grab, Capisce," I barked. "That's what I'm talking about."

The twins were trying to scoot backward using their free foot. All they managed to do was kick up some dust. Capisce barely struggled before letting them loose. "Remind me to atomic twist them later," he growled.

The twins rolled back, bumped into each other, and proceeded to get into a wrestling match.

"Yeah, if they don't kill themselves before you can get 'em.."

Paulie snapped his finger on the back of Lights's head and ran around the tent before collapsing next to me. The Red Sox announcers were wrapping up the loss in voices that bordered on the desperate. This had been the tenth game of a ten game home stand and the Sox had won just three games. Three and seven…3-7…seven loses out of ten! Ugh! Anyway you cut it the result was a stink bomb. Tomorrow was a scheduled off day, but the way their fortunes (or misfortunes I should say), have been going, they had to fly to Texas to make up a rain out game, then go on a ten day, eleven game road trip, ending with a doubleheader in New York. It was shaping up as the biggest collapse our young lives have ever witnessed.

"So, whatta we gonna do?" Paulie said.

Right, back to that. "Where do we stand, Lights?"

Lights was now wrestling with our adopted tailless cat, Twotails. Covered in a gray dust bowl tux, Twotails looked like she had the best of Lights. She pounced on his chest, did a forward roll over his face, and ended with her front paws cuffing both ears. Some of the dirt had fallen off Twotails and a white and black paw showed through. She was so dirty most of the time I had forgotten what her true color was…black… right? I think.

"Tags, give that a cat a bath, she stinks somethin' awful."

Twotails had become mine by default, I suppose. The Beacons' dad wouldn't allow an animal, the Capiscios already had a pet, a very big dog—what else—so I won my parents over by promising no matter what I would take full responsibility in caring for *my* cat. The only problem was my cat never learned to clean herself…*ever*! She was a filthy, dirty, homeless cat when she found us, and she wasn't about to change.

In the faint glow of my parents backyard light, we watched Twotails strut away and look over her shoulder at us as if she had conquered her enemies. With her chest out she disappeared into the bushes…with a baseball batting glove velcroed to the hair on her butt.

"Hey, is that mine?"

"It better not be mine."

"It's not mine, I have mine right…oh, Twotails, ya better run."

BEFORE THEY WERE CHAMPS

The guys were out of control laughing as I waved most likely a final goodbye to my new official Red Sox batting glove.

"Boys, shut the radio off and get inside that tent before the mosquito's eat you alive," my mother said from the kitchen window. "And keep it quiet, people are trying to get some sleep."

"Okay mom."

"Goodnight Mrs. Tags."

"Later Mrs. T."

"Night Mrs. Taglia."

There still were rules that eleven-year-olds had to follow if we were to live another day.

"No sneaking out, either. Once you're in, you're in. Right?"

"Yes ma'am."

"I hear you Mom."

"Absolutemente."

"Yes please."

"Yes please?" We all whispered between laugh snorts. "What's the matter with you, Lights?"

"Go to sleep now," my mom repeated.

We would think no more about sneaking out than we would about eating worms smothered in apple sauce…or would we? We climbed into the tent laughing quietly and about to zip up the flap when Twotails shot through the opening. "My glove," I exclaimed. "You may be filthy, but…but who cares?"

"Let her sit on your head then tell me who cares," laughed Lights.

I settled into my fake sleep, counting the bugs being annihilated by Mr. Sal's bug zapper and contemplated the fate of our Boston Red Sox. The Red Sox needed help…but from where?

"Lights," I whispered, "how may games out are we now?"

"We're 6 1/2 games behind the stinkin' New Yawk Jankeys, and two behind the Orioles. Worse than that, Lefty hasn't won a game in two months. He's 0-3 with five no-decisions. *Five*! How can you have five no-no's?"

"The lousy bullpen, that's how," added Capisce.

"No run support," kicked in Lights.

"So whatta we gonna do, Tags?"

They always looked to me for the answers, and a lot of times I could come up with something to satisfy them, but this problem was going to need some time…and definitely some thought.

"Hey Tags?"

"Yeah Lights."

"After tonight the nights become shorter, less light. We'll be back to school before you can say, 'the Red Sox lose, the Red Sox lose'."

Mister Doomsday strikes again.

TWO

It was Saturday morning, the Red Sox had lost the Thursday makeup game with the Texas Rangers and dropped the opening game of a four game series with Kansas City to go eight games back of the American East leading...*aaahhhh,* it kills me to say it, New York Yankees. Lefty was pitching today—our only hope—but even he had become mediocre, or worse, just another guy.

I had my Saturday morning chores to do; clean my room, empty the kitty litter box which Twotails never used, thank you very much, see if Dad needed any help, (fingers were always crossed when I'd ask). When I was finished (it seemed as if I was the only one with chores) I knew the guys would be waiting in my backyard. I grabbed my "official" score book.

"I'll be at Fenway," I called out. Fenway wasn't the actual Fenway Park. It *was* our gift to ourselves for being the best Red Sox fans that ever lived. Fenway was Capisce's backyard, a perfect fenced in yard that we had changed a bit to look like the real thing. The yard was already shaped like a baseball diamond; two eight-foot high wooden fences divided my house on one side, and the Beacons' house on the other. The fences met at a point at the farthest of the yard; that was our home plate (actually a cover from a plastic trash barrel was the plate. The gray base lines (we used a Mr. Capiscio's lawn spreader filled with a bag of cement we had "borrowed" from my Dad's garage over a year ago, I'm guessing he didn't miss it) ran along the fences with hardly any foul territory, just like at Fenway. Rightfield was the deepest part of Fenway, with tall pine trees lining the section of the fence that angled back in and against Capisce's house. Right center was the back wall of their den and centerfield was an open twenty foot deck, about eight feet high with a three foot lattice fence above that. Leftfield was, well, leftfield was our most proud and creative design. Because Mr. Capiscio owned a hardware store we had our hands on anything we needed. We nailed two, 4'x8' sheets of plywood, onto two round fence posts, and painted the plywood green, like the Green Monster, then painted it as a scoreboard, complete with innings, standings, strikes, balls, and outs. We would lean our Green Monster against the porch and as easy as you could say, "knockout," Fenway was born. The outfielder was in charge of writing in the score using white chalk. The ball we used was a regulation Wiffle Ball, with the hard plastic on one side and the holes on the other. The rules were simple. We used a pitch back machine behind home plate, the kind with the netting pulled tight and the square strike zone. We counted walks and strikeouts, but there wasn't any running of the bases. Except for home runs, where we'd try to "out style" the other on our home run trot. Capisce had a double-arm pinwheel trot that was pretty lame but definitely unique. Paulie ran shaking his head as if to say "ya can't get me out" and touched the bases with a sideways skip. Lights sprinted around the bases, ending with a leap and double foot whammy on home plate. Mine was a slow, and I mean s-l-o-w, head-bobbing-arm-pumping-side-stepping-trash-talking victory trot. Of course, mine was the most knockout. Any ball hit to right that wasn't hit into the pine trees was an automatic out. Off the right-center field wall below the window was a double, above the window a triple. Off the wall below the score a double, above a triple. Any ball hit on the porch a round tripper. If a ball got by the outfielder on the ground it was a single. Any ball on the ground touched, even if it wasn't handled cleanly, went as an out.

"Who's who today, Tagsarino?" The boys were playing catch and arguing about something. They all had on their white Red Sox shirts. I had on my red.

"It's you and me, Lights. You better go home and put on your red because we're the home team today."

"I told ya numb skull. He wouldn't listen to me…he wouldn't," Paulie said disgustingly.

"Are you sure?"

"Of course he's sure," Capisce added. "We were on the same team yesterday."

In these times of confusion, anarchy, and mutiny, so to speak, I had my trusty score book. Every game I charted; the teammates, the home team, the hits, the pitching line, and the scores. I opened the book to yesterday's happenings. "Quiet… let me read from *the* book"

"We must have quiet," yelled Capisce.

"Yes, quiet amongst the peasants," laughed Lights.

"All heel as the book is read," shouted Paulie as he knelt.

I read the statistics in a Kingly manner…then laughed so hard I snorted out a booger.

"Ahhh, gross."

"Tags!"

"I'm not on *your* team today."

We were still laughing as Lights headed home to change into his home red jersey. "Wear your Hilberto Otto "35", I yelled, and we hopped the fence into the Capisce's backyard. I had been up all night working on a plan (I must say, it seemed out-of-this-world knockout late last night) that I thought might turn the Red Sox' sinking season around.

* * *

Saturday was baseball, more baseball, still more baseball, then baseball for desert. If the sun shone for twenty-four hours then we would've played baseball the whole day. My dad tried to sell me on a story that the sun on a part of Alaska did not set from May until August.

"No way," the Beacons' declared. "All day?"

"I know," I said. "Imagine that, all day and nothing but sun."

"It's true, look it up," said Capisce. "I had to do a book report on the Alaskan Natives for Mr. Reedy. They were called, The Natives of the Midnight Sun, and where they lived. Hey, don't look at me like I'm nuts, it's a fact. Sun and nuthin' but sun for four months."

"Get out…knockout."

"Knockout is right. All day?"

"All day."

We all agreed we wished we were born in Alaska and lived there our whole life so we could just play baseball until we grew old and died. That would've been so knockout we didn't have a word for it.

Of course one us had to ruin the thought with a stupid fact. It was Paulie.

"If they get to play baseball *alllll* day, then how come there's no big league ballplayers that we know of that are Alaskanans?"

"I think it's Alaskians."

"No, just Alaskans."

"Does it matter? Who says they do play all day?"

"Yeah, maybe they can't."

"That would be really dumb, dumber than dumb. Tags, give me a word for major dumb."

"Dumb-a-rooney."

"Exactly."

"My grandfather said nobody in the world had better eyesight than Ted Williams. He told me he could see a mosquito on a flea from one-hundred yards. I'll bet you they have great vision, like Ted Williams."

"Probably for day games only, though. Maybe they can't see at night?"

So we agreed before the first pitch that we'd all be in the Hall of Fame if we were raised in Alaska and played only day games.

Mrs. Capisce brought us all lemonade as we lounged in the shade in right field under the cover of the pine trees. It must've been 100 degrees in the sun today. We had the second game to play on our scheduled Saturday doubleheader so we had to rest to regain our strength.

"We kicked some serious buttski in the first, huh Tags?"

"11 to 7? I wouldn't call that serious, Lights," grumbled Capisce.

"Ah, it was never as close as the final score."

The time was now. "Listen up ya knuckleheads, I got a plan."

"Don't forget to give me credit for a triple, Tags, not a double," complained Paulie.

"I got it. You guys gonna listen?" I had the sense that their complete attention, miraculously, was centered on my plan. "I might have a plan, an idea on how we can help the Sox."

THREE

Lefty had pitched better today but still received a no-decision in a Red Sox 8-5 win.

"That's six no-no's. Un-bee-leave-able," said Capisce.

We were lying around my backyard after supper keeping bug-zapping score and weighing what we had to lose compared to what we had to gain. We definitely had more to lose, like our pass to be kids. We were facing permanent grounded for life verdicts, if we got caught. But we were talking about the Red Sox, *our* Red Sox and some gambles were worth the guilty verdicts.

"But we're all in, right?"

"Of course we're all in," Capisce added. "It's all or nuthin' like in everything we do."

"I have just one question. It's sort of a big one, though, like the big cosmic risk," grimaced Lights. "I'm still in, just got a question." Lights paused and lowered his voice. "How are we going to get there and back without our parents wondering where we are? I'm guessing it's going to take a couple of days."

"Never mind that, how *are* we gonna get there?" added Paulie.

Yeah, how are we gonna get there? "Don't worry about getting there, you leave that to me." I hadn't exactly ironed out all the wrinkles of the trip yet, but I was getting close. As far as what to tell the parents…

"I know, we tell them we're joining the circus and this is our innish, innish…"

"Initiation."

"Right. And we have to travel for a week without our parents so as to learn how to live alone and survive."

"Lights, I dunno…where do you come up with these ideas?" Capisce snapped Lights on the top of his head with his finger.

"C'mon Lights, Mom and Dad aren't gonna let us run away with a circus. Do you see a circus around here anyway? I don't think so."

"Well, maybe not a circus…"

"Yeah, maybe not a circus," I interrupted, "but something like that."

"That's what I'm talking about it, something like that," Lights said proudly.

"Somethin' like what? No matter what, our parents are gonna give us the third degree. 'Who's in charge? Who's going? Where ya going?' Am I right?" Capisce grabbed Twotails as if he was asking for her approval.,

"You're right. That's why what Lights said gave me an idea." I rolled off my back and sat up excitingly. The guys saw me and followed suit. Most great thinkers, Einstein, Da Vinci, Darwin, their ideas were like tiny waves that over time became huge tsunami's. Time only improved plans or ideas… or made them seem really, really dumb. I like to think mine was becoming a brilliant tsunami, a plan unmatched by any mere other 'great thinker'. "Okay guys, listen up. I think what Lights said might not be so far off." I watched Lights look at Capisce and Paulie and nod his head as if to say, 'see, I ain't that dumb'. "It might be a little twisted, but it ain't that bad." You see, that's what good friends are all about. You allow them to crow a bit, then when the time's right, you put them back in their place. "When Lights said circus I was thinking… Camp Billow."

"Camp Billow? That's for babies. Our parents aren't going to believe we're going on a trip with Camp Billow."

"You're right, Capisce. But we're not going to be the ones going. We're the ones *taking* the ones going."

"Say what?"

"They're always looking for extra volunteers to watch the kids on trips, right? Well, we sign up, but not really, we just tell our parents we signed up. Once we say we're signed up, then we can take off at any time, for a couple of days, which is probably all we need to get there and back, before the parentals freak. We pack for a hiking trip…that's what we'll say, we're going hiking. Capisce, you have to get extra batteries and stuff from your dad's store. Anyway, that's what we'll tell them. We'll go over everything we need before the trip."

"But that's lying, Tags. My parents are gonna know I'm lying."

"Leave that up to me Lights. I'll talk to Mom and Dad…the story part. We don't really have to lie."

"Ah, Tags? Once we get there whatta we tell this Spaceman guy?" Lights looked at me and shook his head.

What every true, red, white and blue-blooded fan of the

Boston Red Sox would ask, "please come to Boston, our hopeless team needs you?" I said.

"And if that doesn't work we kidnap the old guy. Do ya think he can still pitch?"

I believed Capisce meant what he said.

* * *

The rain cut short our hang in my backyard so we all agreed to head home and make a personal list of things needed for our trip, at least a weeks worth, and meet tomorrow in my yard by 9 a.m. sharp with list in hand. I'd said goodnight to my parents, complaining with mom about school shopping and dad about the Red Sox. I got on my computer and checked the distance from Belmont, MA to Craftsbury, VT—210 miles. I had a lot of work to do to get us there.

* * *

"I made my list last night. Most of the stuff I can get at my dad's store. Batteries, bug spray…"

"Oh yeah, bug spray. Good one Capisce."

"Get the rub on, it's better than the spray, too much alcohol."

"I'll get everyone a rub on. We'll need eats, too. My dad keeps jars of Beef Jerky and lollipops at the counter. I'll woof a bunch of everything."

"I'm bringing my desk radio so we can listen to the games. Me and Paulie are packing most of our new camping stuff, like the frying pans and stove."

"Good idea, Lights. If that's the deal, why don't we borrow a few eggs each? Not enough to make our mothers suspicious, though. Be sure to make some sandwiches, too. We'll say

Camp Billow asked for each chaperone to bring some food." I liked the way our plan was going.

"We'll need your tent Tags." Capisce was wrestling with Twotails and because of the rain last night was covered in mud from the cat's paws.

"Are we leaving today?" Lights looked as if his eyeballs were going to pop out of his head.

"No, not today. We have to pack, get the stuff from our lists, and talk our parents into letting us go on the Camp Billow trip. Whatta ya say we take a group vote? I say next Sunday, one week from today." I thrust my arm out and waited for the guys to knuckle me in solidarity…or not. One by one we met in the circle knuckle smack.

"Sunday morning it is."

FOUR

Twotails ran in circles chasing her tail that didn't exist. I figured it must've been like a phantom tail, something she must've thought was still attached to her. The circles became tighter and quicker until she lost her balanced and collapsed on her side chugging like an ancient steam engine. Her eyes closed and she slept. "Geez Twotails, if you put an eighth of that effort into cleaning yourself you'd be a knockout cat."

I watched her sleep then turned my attention to the posters of the Red Sox hanging on my wall.

They were what my dad called "heroes that will just break your heart." I wanted so much to prove him wrong . On my wall was a poster size Red Sox schedule. Every game I marked in the score in a box next to the game number. Today was the one-hundredth and seventh game of the year with fifty-five games remaining. With the season winding down my dad's words were gaining strength. They had won today, but so had the Yankees. The battle was on, the deficit remained at eight games, Lefty's game was off, the fans were growing impatient, and the new school year was looming. "Oh brother, Twotails, if that doesn't bum ya out I don't know what will." I wrote in the score and sat back to gaze at the Red Sox posters. The players were tacked up in a diamond shape to represent their positions. "I haven't given up on you like some…yet.," First base, Bo Henry; second, Hal Wallace; short, Lee Lozcaino; third, Tony Palagrini; left, Hilberto Otto; center, Stanley Dupree; right, Grady Telinger; catching, Steve Berano; and pitching, number 18, Lefty Van Weller. Lefty's poster shot was of him throwing a curve ball on the outside corner of the plate for a third strike. That big breaking pitch could freeze the best hitters in the league. The pitch to left handed batters would look like it was going straight for their noggin' then disappear to the outside corner of home plate. To right handed hitters the pitch looked as if it was heading for the first base dugout then bite the black on the outside of home plate. He was awesome, I thought. "He *was* awesome," I said to Twotails who was purring away. "We just have to get him back to awesome." And that was where The Spaceman had to come through for us and the usual suffering fans of Red Sox Nation.

I brought up Spaceman's stats on my computer and knew he was the guy to help Lefty get back on his game. Maybe Spaceman didn't have Hall-of-Fame stats, but he was the best left handed pitcher the Sox ever had (alive, at least) that knew how to pitch in Fenway Park. With his sweeping curve ball coming out of the bleachers in right center it made hitting almost impossible. I believe Lefty just forgot how to pitch at Fenway.

"You gotta help us Spaceman," and I emailed him for the one-hundredth time. And for the 100th time I knew he wouldn't reply. "We're just gonna have to come see you Spaceman. We're on our way." I didn't have a clue where he lived, but how hard could it be? "We just look for an old guy with a long white beard and long hair working on a farm in Craftsbury," I said to Twotails. She lifted her head off my carpet to look at me. Her eyes shifted from me to the wall then back at me before she returned to her sleep. If she could've talked her words would've been, "HA, ARE YOU OUT OF YOUR MIND?" And I would've replied, "DESPERATE TIMES CALL FOR DESPERATE MEASURES." Or something like that.

   I charted our statistics in the "official" score book and closed the book before turning out the lights. Tomorrow was the beginning of a long week of planning, and lying to our parents (I much prefer not exactly telling the truth to lying, that sounded to…to grown-up. A kid could still get away with "sort of not telling the truth," an adult lied). Tomorrow I'd tell the guys how we were going to get there, to Vermont, at least three quarters of how. The last part, like how we were going to find him, well, the guys *did* like surprises. We were kids after all, you know.

FIVE

"Red jersey today, Lights." The guys were waiting for me as usual.

Lights grunted, threw his glove down and ran home to change. "I told him, but…"

"I know." We waited for Lights and tossed the ball around in atypical silence. There was no teasing of Lights, laughing at a filthy Twotails, or talking about statistics. We were like professionals with our game face on—all serious and stuff. Lights bolted around the corner of my house with his "18" red Lefty Van Weller Red Sox shirt on backwards. "Van Weller" was stitched shoulder to shoulder across the front. We all looked at each other than at Lights and burst out laughing and tossing insults like fastballs at him.

"I know, I know. It's on backward."

"What is wrong with you little brother?"

"I did it on purpose, give you guys a laugh."

"Sure ya did, knucklebrain." Capisce had him in a very weak bear hug.

"No really, I did. And we're twins, Paulie, so I'm not your little brother."

"Yup, by a whole minute. Just go ask mom."

"Let him go Capisce so we can go. We have a bunch of plans to go over…"

"Who's the home team today?"

* * *

I muscled up, all eighty-five pounds of solid rock, and hit a walk-off two run home run to straight away center field for the win. It was a majestic home run, a Picasso blast, a stop-the-clock-did-you see-that masterpiece (in my humble opinion, of course). I did a slow, and I mean s-l-o-w, head-bobbing-arm-pumping-side-stepping-trash-talking victory trot around the bases before leaping on top of Lights and of course Twotails at home plate. The hit was my first walk-off home run of the year and I was going to enjoy it to the max.

"You the bomb, Tags." Lights kept slapping me until I had to plead for him to stop.

"Nice one Tags…"

"Yeah, nice one," Paulie and Capisce said halfheartedly.

I flexed my arm muscles in a body builder's pose before settling comfortably in the shade. "Is there anything sweeter than the home run trot?" Twotails sat proudly next to me… then ran off to attack Lights.

"Yeah, me hitting one," Capisce grumbled.

* * *

We sat in the shade soaking in the still late-morning comfort of a day heading towards a hot and humid finish. Our plan was to play another game, but the looks on my friend's faces were of content to lay in the shade and do a summer nothing.

"You guys up for a summer nothing?" I sipped ice cold water out of the hose we had hooked up to Capisce's backyard faucet, letting the water cool me down before passing it along. "A little nuttin'-nuttin' wouldn't hurt."

"Yeah, it's gettin' hot anyway."

"Might give us a chance to, you know, dizzcuss," Lights said quietly while squirting Twotails.

"Hurry up with the hose, Paulie, will ya? I'm dyin' ovah heah."

"I just saw that movie, it was knockout."

"It's like a hundred years old."

"What? A movie gotta be less than a year old to be good?"

"Maybe. I'm just sayin' anything older than your father is old."

"What movie are you guys talkin' about?" I stretched out in the grass with my arms behind my head and didn't want to be any other place with any other friends talking about any other thing but what we were talking about now—even if I didn't know what the heck we were talking about.

"Hey, my father's young."

"Your father's like forty. Whatta ya call that? I call it o-l-d."

"I don't care, I still say it was a good movie."

"What movie?" I watched a cloud form that looked like the face of my soon-to-be eighth grade teacher, Mrs. Hacker. It frightened me that I was seeing my teacher's face in cloud forms. It also frightened me my teacher's name was Hacker. The cloud formed into a running buffalo and thankfully Mrs. Hacker disappeared.

"Dog Day Afternoon, like today."

"That's more like a billion years old. Were there even color

TV's then?" I threw my batting glove at Paulie but as usual Twotails was in the way and the velcro once again stuck to her like a sticky burr. She bounded off with the glove paddling her like a naughty kid. "Send lawyers, guns and money, Dad, I've been robbed again." I cared not, though, my running buffalo cloud was now a sleek car...a corvette convertible.

Our few seconds of silence (a lifetime for us) watching Twotails was interrupted by a megaton Capisce belch.

"Whoa, *awesome.*"

"*Getout.* Supreme knockout."

"Heavens to mergatroy *knockout* supreme."

We all took turns trying to duplicate Capisce's classic rip. I belched a whopper just as Mrs. Capiscio yelled at us (me) from the deck, "Boys, boys, act like gentlemen."

"Yeah Tags," whispered Lights, "act like a gentleman."

It was time to share my plan with the guys.

"Camp Billow has two buses leaving the high school parking lot Friday morning. The camp is having a weekend nature thing hiking trip to New Hampshire. This is our chance to get away without making our parents worried, so we have to talk to our parents tonight about letting us go."

"Whatta we tell them?"

"Tell them...tell them we ran into Mr. Wallace, the science teacher. And he mentioned how the camp needed volunteers to help chaperone..."

"What *does* that word mean?" Paulie asked.

"It means to keep someone from doing something stupid." Lights shot a "how's that" glance at me.

"Yeah, Lights is right. It's our job to keep the little brats in line."

"How old are these kids?" Capisce asked nervously.

"I dunno, like seven or eight. But what difference does

make? It doesn't matter, 'cause it's not as if we gotta take care of them. We just have to convince our *parents* we gotta take care of them. You guys following me?"

"Yeah, of course."

"Without a doubt."

"I hear ya Tags."

"Okay. So we convince them it would be a learning experience, a grown-up responsible thing that Mr. Wallace says will help us in science class next year. Pretty good, huh?"

"You're pretty good with this lying…I don't know if I…we are." Lights pointed at himself and his brother.

"Don't worry so much, Lights. If they let us go they'll never know we lied."

Capisce lowered his voice and looked up at the porch deck to see if the coast was clear. "This is BIG, guys. Think about it. If we pull this off, get Spaceman to actually help Lefty, we'll be heroes—our parents will be heroes for having heroes. How can they be mad at us even *if* they find out we sort of kind of lied? They couldn't punish us…well, they *could*, but that would make them look like they hate the Sox, like they were Yankee fans, and nobody likes Yankee fans. If Spaceman helps Lefty, you know he'll give us all the credit because… because he's The Spaceman and he's cool and he couldn't care less about things like credit and I know for a fact he hates the Yankees. He major knockout hates the Jan-kees. He *is* the Spaceman. Am I right?"

"Capisce is right, nobody likes Jan-key fans."

I hadn't thought of that angle, nor did I believe in it, either. Our parents could punish us until the sun goes down in Alaska if they felt it was proper and no one would write one letter in our defense. They were after all, our PARENTS! We weren't getting punished for our attempt to help the Sox, we were going to get fried for lying. "That's right, they won't punish us, no one likes the Yankees, especially their loud mouthed fans," I lied.

"Ha, they might even make statues of us in front of Fenway Park."

"Just imagine…I'm standing with my Black Cobra bat on my shoulder. Tags, you're windin' up and throwin' a pea right at me. Paulie, you're crunched down at shortstop. And Lights, you're ready to run back and watch my home run go *way* over your head. Those statues will be in front of Fenway, forever. How can our parents punish *us*?"

"How come they make *you* the hero? Way over my head…" Lights scoffed.

"Maybe the statues should be the four of us on horses—like those guys, you know from Notre Dame, The Four Horseman. Now those guys were BIG!" Paulie said proudly.

"Who cares about four guys from…"

"Guys, will ya? Forget about the statues. We have to find our way up to Vermont first, then find The Spaceman, then talk him into…"

"Or kidnap him," muttered Capisce. "You *are* aware the Jan-kees series starts Friday night."

"We're not kidnaping him, Capisce, I don't think we could. And yeah, we know the Yankees series starts Friday. Anyway, we tell him how Lefty needs his help and without him the teams' season is finished. He probably knows how bad things are…he still follows his old team, right? " Then how come he never answered my emails? I thought. Maybe he doesn't care. But how could that be? The thought never entered my mind, because the thought of *not* caring about the Red Sox was an impossibility. You're born, you care. You wear the uniform, you definitely care. You go to heaven, you care for eternity.

"I bet ya we could kidnap him."

"Will you forget about the kidnap, Capisce."

"I'm just sayin'…he *is* an old man."

"No one's kidnaping anyone. We're going up there to talk to him about talking to Lefty, that's it, that's all. Maybe we can get him to straightened him out."

"So I guess I can leave my duct tape at home?" Capisce looked down then started to laugh

"No, bring it," Lights joked. "We'll tape you to a tree."

"Oh, ya will?" Capisce faked as if he was going to get after Lights and Lights bolted to the front yard. "You better run." Capisce grabbed the water hose to squirt Lights but he had gotten out of range as quick as a cat.

"C'mon. C'mon, guys. Lights get back here," I pleaded.

Lights returned and we lounged in the little shade the backyard offered us and talked about the week ahead. We all made our lists in our heads of things to carry. "So we leave on Friday morning," I reminded them.

"And we come back Sunday afternoon," we agreed. "Or ya can forget about the statues," we agreed in four-part harmony.

"Hey, Paulie said 'dame,'" snickered Lights.

SIX

Dear Mr. Spaceman,
I've always been a big fan of yours ever since I could remember. Of course, I'm way too young to remember when you pitched because I'm only eleven (I'll be twelve in October), but because of the internet and cable television I've seen you pitch, and I think you're knockout (that means good). Me and my friends, we all think you're super-knockout. We think you had the best curve ball that any pitcher ever, \ever had, especially when you were at Fenway. You probably know the Red Sox are not doing that great because you still must follow them. In fact, they're heading for the you-know-what as usual. Every year they do this to us, but I don't have to tell you. Me and my friends think this year could be different. They have the hitting, no one's better than Hilberto Otto and Stanley Dupree. Their defense up the middle with Lozaino and Wallace is awesome. The problem is the lefty pitcher, Lefty Van Weller. That's where you come in. We think you can help him find himself. My friend, Capisce, thinks his shoulder's

opening up too much. Lights thinks he's not following through. Paulie thinks he's tipping off his pitches. I think he's just, well, thinking too much. He's making something that was easy, hard. You would know better, much, much better, than we would. This is why we have to talk to you, and have you talk to Lefty. Me and my friends are on our way up to see you. I'm not too sure how we're going to find you, but we're hoping we will, and then you can come back with us and talk to Lefty. The season is getting late and the Red Sox need our help. We hope to see you Saturday.

Your fans,
Tags, Lights, Paulie, and Capisce (and Twotails).

SEVEN

The week had had that nervous feel, like the head-pounding, stomach-churning kind of week before a big math test that you knew you had no chance in acing. It was Monday morning only yesterday, and now as I opened my eyes and rubbed the sleep out of them I stared at my Red Sox wall calendar and my stomach felt like a rookie stepping into the batter's box for the first time—today was Friday, today was The Day, today was Test Day. The week hadn't scooted bye, heck, it had *flown* bye. If this was "give Tags a prize week," the pace would've been slower than Big Hilberto Otto going from first to third on a single. Twotails jumped from the floor and landed on my knotted stomach, her face was covered in dust. "Not now Twotails." I tossed the filthy cat off my bed and lay motionless and noted fifty-two games remained on the Red Sox schedule. Miraculously the Sox had picked up two games this week and were now tried with the Orioles and within six of the Yankees. "There's no turning back now, Twotails. It's now or never," I tossed the sheet aside and sat up in bed. "It's one for all and all for one. Time is at…time is at…is," I was running out of cliches. "It's every man for himself." When all else failed quoting the Three Stooges was a quick and easy escape. I had managed to perk up my belief into thinking this wonderfully farfetched idea might just work. "You never know Twotails, I bet going to Mars sounded dumb at the time, and now look, it's like going to the mall." I headed to the bathroom but stopped first at my computer. What do I have to lose, I smirked, as I checked my emails. "Yeah, not today, like the one-hundred and…" my mouth dropped and my heart stopped. Could it be? "I don't believe it, I don't stinkin' bee-leave-it!" I read the email three times before printing it to show the guys. "He'll meet with us, Twotails. He finally agrees they need help and he sees his duty and he'll do it. I told you all along he's been paying attention. Alright…KNOCKOUT!" I ran to get ready for the trip.

EIGHT

Mom and dad fought with me tooth and nail about driving us to the bus to kiss us off for the big trip but I held my ground and convinced them that by walking there it would be our first real test of independence and slow acceptance into "grown-up land." My dad would call that a bunch of "stronzate," I'd call that a bunch of stronzate, too, but stronzate that works in my favor. Whatever you call it, *it* worked, as I hugged my parents goodbye and scampered out with Twotails glued to my ankle. The guys were waiting eagerly as I thundered into Capisce's backyard. Backpacks and other stuff were strewn around the yard while the guys played a game of catch. We all wore our Lefty Van Weller jersey. A fine decision, I thought proudly. When they saw me they tossed their gloves aside and ran over to get the scoop.

"What it say? What did he say?"

"Yeah, yeah, c'mon, Tags, what'd he say?"

"I knew he'd answer us. Didn't I say that?"

"You're full of you-know-what Lights You never in your life said that."

"Yeah I did. Tell 'em Tags how I said I bet he answers us one of these days."

I knew after I hung out my window and whispered to Lights about the email that I probably shouldn't have. "He actually did say that, really. But then I told *you* not to say anything, remember? I wanted to surprise them." I flung my backpack with the others and took the printed email out of my pocket.

"Yesssss," Capisce exclaimed.

"Sorry Tags," Lights said. "But read it, Tags-o-tags-o-buddy-of-mine. Read it loud."

"This is knockout. I can't wait. I'm gonna burst my guts and cover you guys with, like, all gross stuff and things." Paulie pretended to throw up then belly-flopped onto our traveling packs.

"Hey ya knucklehead, watch it. I got bags of chips and stuff in there."

"Yeah, me too. I don't want to be starving out in the wild with nothing to eat but squashed chips. Remember the party that went across the country and almost froze to death…they had nothin' but donuts to eat, then ran out of them and had to eat each other? No way I'm munchin' on you. Disgusting."

"Donuts?"

"Yes, donuts," Lights smirked. "I think that's what they became known as, the donut party, somethin'…or somethin' like that."

"Oh geez."

I shook my head and began to read to get their attention…
Dear guys,

Thank you very much for being such big fans, I never get tired of hearing that, and you boys being so young, well, that means even more to me! That's, well, we had a saying when I was growing up—very hip, very cool! Right on! I truly appreciate the kind words. I did have a pretty hip curve, that's the truth. As far as the Sox go, I wouldn't get too nervous, yet. Six games out with fifty-two to go isn't insurmountable, but I hear your concern. I've seen Lefty pitch but haven't studied him. What I have noticed is perhaps his shoulder's opening up too soon...

"Ah-ha," proclaimed Capisce.

...or maybe he's not following through...

"What I tell ya?" said Lights

...with his delivery. There's an outside chance he could be tipping his pitches...

"Outside chance? I still think that's the reason he stinks right now," buzzed Paulie.

...or like you mentioned, Tags, maybe just thinking too much and not doing with what comes naturally, p-i-t-c-h-i-n-g. You boys seem to know your baseball, which means you all could be right on.

Talking to Lefty could help, then again, the cows could stay out all night and who would know? Am I right...?

"Huh?" asked Lights.

"Sshhh, Lights. Go on Tags, will he see us?"

But, I don't leave my farm much anymore. That doesn't mean, though, I couldn't meet you guys. It's just that, I'm not really sure giving you my address is the safest or smartest move. I'll tell you what? There's a restaurant on Rt.14 just outside of Craftsbury, it's called the Craftsbury Inn and Restaurant. Why don't you guys meet me there Saturday for lunch? Buying a few fans lunch if not solving the Red Sox woes is the least I can do. So, I'll see you Saturday.

Have a safe trip,

BEFORE THEY WERE CHAMPS

Spaceman

"He'll see us? He'll see us! Knockout! We better get moving." Capisce started scooping up the bags and walking out of the yard.

"Capisce, we should double check and make sure we have everything we need. Once we get moving there's no turning back."

We went over the list like surgeons before a life-saving operation. Everything seemed to be in order, including packages of dry cat food for Twotails. She was coming with us unless I chained her and tied her up with duct tape in my cellar. And I could never do that to her because she'd figure out a way to get even with me when I returned. So we checked her off our list.

"I'll read, you guys say check. Got it?"

"Got it."

* * *

And I read: sleeping bags, stove, Sterno, lighter, radio, batteries, milk, butter, cheese and crackers, bread, hot dogs (my idea), chips, sodas, water, juice, beef jerky, and gloves and a ball.

"We're right and ready."

"All accounted for Captain Tags."

"Now can we go?"

"Capisce, *now* we can go."

Like we had done these maneuvers countless times, we hiked up gear and our courage and bounded out of our peaceful surroundings to save the Red Sox from certain disgrace.

"Grounded for life, you know," I said to no one.

"Or maybe just 'till college," added Paulie.

NINE

We cut through the closed elementary school parking lot, down a hill where the town pool was (also closed), and forcibly slithered with all of our gear under a wooden fence that was also the fence to Belmont's long-ago town dump. The dump had been out of service as far back as when my dad was a kid. He told me him and his buddies used to play baseball in the dump. But I'd bet you all the money you had their field was no where as knockout as ours…not even close.

"Once we go past the dump we can cut across Concord Avenue and onto the train tracks," I reminded them. "But, let's miss the tunnel, deal?"

The guys answered as one, "ohyeahnoproblemihearyaforsureyounoitiwasthinkingthat." Ah, the tunnel. The town's old timers had sewn tapestries of tales passed down through generations of creatures—actually one creature—that lived in the tunnel and ate kids. He was half human and half rat that only came out of the tunnel in the searing heat to hunt for fresh meat. "Never go close to the opening of the tunnel," we were told, "or he'll grab you, slice you in half and eat all of your insides before you can cry 'mom.'" He had lived in the tunnel for two hundred years and although no one had actually come face to face with Ratso Risoli, old folklore was enough to keep us from crossing the tunnel opening. Someday, I promised, I'll have to go in the tunnel to find out for myself. Maybe, just maybe, I'll talk the guys into following me in?

"Hey Tags, you know what? When we get back remind me to remind one of you guys that we should build a field in here."

"Yeah, my dad played in here, Lights. We should make that a most-definitely."

"I second that most-definitely."

"Oh yeah, make it a third."

"Absolutamental."

"And, I think I know where, too." Climbing around all the rusting junk piled high, past an ancient milk truck and over discarded appliances was another fence that bordered the dump. On the other side was where I envisioned to be our home away from home. "I realize where our field is now is pretty knockout, but wait until I show you this. I came over here one day when I was bored—you guys were away, or somethin'—then I remembered my dad telling me about a field his friends built when he was our age. I don't know how I ever found it. They hid the place, or more like the place hid itself. The field's kinda overgrown with weeds, but it definitely has good-look potential."

"Like Haley Bailey, Paulie's girrrlllllfriend?"

"She's not my girlfriend, ya donkey's diaper."

"She'll be wearing next year, mark my word," added Capisce.

"Who cares, she's not my girlfriend."

"You better make her your girlfriend, she's smokin'." Lights pretended putting out a smoke on his rear then mimicked a girl's voice. "I love you Paulie, with all my heart…my big strong boyyyyfriend." We all laughed as Lights strolled around shaking his rear with his hands up his shirt to imitate breasts. "Haley Bailey, the girl Paulie…dateies."

"The girl what? That's the worst rhyme in the history of the world."

"*The* worst."

Lights even agreed and snorted, "lame-o if I don't say so myself."

"We better leave all our stuff out here. Anyway, we gotta cut through down there," I pointed along the fence where it disappeared around a bend. "We can get onto the train tracks from around there and avoid the tunnel opening and ole' Ratso. Help me grab this board."

"I got it Tags."

The way in was two pieces of wooden planks that swung up as if hinged. Twotails bolted past as I stepped through the fence and onto the field followed by the guys. The excitement rush I felt was like I just drank a dozen sodas.

"Awesome," I said.

"This is gonna be incredible," added Lights.

"Very knockout," Paulie sighed.

"Knockout to the zillionth degree," said Capisce.

Amen, we all added. It *was* knockout. The field was bordered on the base line sides with fence. Left field had a brick wall that must have been the side of the warehouse that was the old dump's offices. The wall had Green Monster practically written on it. Center field and right field had trees that stood sixty feet high, perfect for knocking down high line drives. The weeds and grass were up to our hips but we could tell once we flattened and cut the stuff down we had all to ourselves the most knockout spot for a ball field.

"Another time, guys, we should get rolling." We soaked in the possibilities, visualizing the layout of the field, commenting on the brick wall and how that would be our left field and *our* Green Monster like Fenway Park's famous wall. I had an overwhelming feeling we'd be spending a great deal of time next year on this little spit of land inside the dump (of all places). "If they don't turn it into million dollar condo's and yuppie ice cream shops," I said out loud.

"Turn what into what?"

"Nah, I was just thinking out loud."

"I say we have a sit down strike if they come here with the bulldozers. We'll tie Lights to a tree with duct tape. They won't dare cut you down." Capisce punched Lights on the shoulder and high-fived me as we made our way through the fence. "There's always innocence lost during war. Am I right, or am I right?"

"Whoa, very impressive Capisce. When'd you get so smart?"

"Blueberries, my man, blueberries. I've been eatin' them by the bushel. They're suppose to increase the blood flow to your brain and better your memory. I'm walkin' proof."

Paulie was first to the fence and halfway through making it an automatic because of "getaway advantage" that he'd toss the first insult at Capisce. He was sure his back leg was coming through the rickety fence before the insult was hurled. We're kids remember, and kids have rules of engagement like adults do. Rule number one is when insulting a bigger foe always have a clear and easy escape route previously laid out in your head…always.

"To better your memory Capisce, ya gotta *have* a brain first, right?" Paulie saw Capisce make a move toward the opening and he bolted letting the loose fence slam back

"You're toast, Beacon." Capisce pushed the fence open and what happened next goes back to the kids' rules of engagement. Chapter and verse number one—easy escape route. As Lights and I laughed, (under our breath, of course), we heard a loud thud as the board went up and struck something that sounded like a ball on a bat. The board came down as quick as a blink of an eye. We heard Paulie call out in pain.

"Oh man, did ya kill Paulie?" Lights held his breath as we fought over each other to get to the fence for first dibs on the casualty report. We couldn't get past Capisce as he stood solidly, looked at us with a "oh geez" glare, turned, took a deep breath and pushed on the board slowly and carefully. He peeked through the slat…and started to laugh.

I squeezed by Capisce as Lights pulled on my shirt to get a look. Paulie was lying in a heap, twisted and tangled and tied up in all of our equipment. He had bolted through the fence and forgotten about the camping equipment tossed all over the grass. Paulie had failed, failed miserably in his assessment of the escape route. By my view his failed assessment probably cost him a couple of hours of sitting comfort.

"Oh boy, that'll teach you, ya knucklehead," laughed Capisce.

"Let me tell you, that looks *painful*."

"Whoa brother, how to go, leading with your head." Lights grabbed his gut and doubled over laughing. "He ain't sittin' for *hours*."

Paulie lay on his side massaging his bum. His head was turned away from us but I could tell by the red color of his ear he was holding both his breath and his tears inside. I figured he tripped over the pile of camping stuff, and while getting to his feet must've leaned over at the wrong time...at the worst time.

"Go ahead and laugh ya jerks, it ain't funny...it hurt."

"Oh, it's funny," we all added.

"C'mon Paulie, you'll be fine." I went through the fence and bent down next to him. "We better get going. You alright?"

"Yeah, yeah, I guess. Was there a nail in the board?" Paulie slowly got to his feet, the red color of his face starting to subside. "I guess we're even Capisce?"

"*I'd* say we were," he laughed. "What happened?"

"I dunno. I tripped over my stuff...failed the number one rule of engagement. When I went to get up, ba-boom, in the keystah." Even Paulie saw the humor now and began to laugh while still rubbing his sore area. "That was harder than any baseball Capisce has hit all year."

"Not even close," argued Capisce. "I've had tons of harder hits than that."

We all agreed (well, three of us agreed under our breath that it was the biggest hit of the year), he'd definitely hit tons harder than that, but Hilberto Otto sure would've been proud of that one. Capisce finished with a Red Sox announcer Downtown Davey's home run call, "tell it sooooooo long everyyyyyybodddddy."

"Knockout. Let's get moving guys. I want to show you the map I printed out of where the train goes. We gotta get to this area by...what time is it Lights?"

Lights had the most awesomest wristwatch. Taking a mighty swing in the center of the watch was the Red Sox designated hitter, Louie Cardinale. When you pushed in a button on the side of the watch, the sound of the bat cracking a baseball and then a roar of the crowd would begin, then Louie Cardinale would read the time.

"It's 9:07...LC time."

We loved to hear Louis Cardinale, or LC to us, read the time so much we'd drive Lights batty by constantly asking him the time. Even better was when twelve o'çlock struck. A roar of the crowd then a crack of the bat would sound, then a tiny LC would scamper around the bases like he'd hit a home run as the crowd roared. Sometimes when we were bored we'd make Lights wind the time to twelve o'clock just to hear the crowd go crazy. Hearing the crowd roar was knockout, driving Lights cuckoo was, well, knockout-a-rooney

"We have to get on the train by at least 9:45. It's probably gonna take us two, three hours, maybe more with stops to get to White River Junction. Then from there…"

"Whoa, whoa, whoa., Train? How we gonna get on a train? Don't we need tickets, which means money? I didn't bring enough money." Lights stopped short and threw up his arms.

"You sound like a train. No money needed on this train ride, Lights."

"Huh?"

"Yeah, huh?" echoed his brother.

These are the reasons I don't divulge *all* of my ideas of a plan before the proper time. "Do you know how, when we cut the tracks, and we see the boxcars or flats just sitting there, and we always say how easy it would be, and how knockout, too, if we jumped on and went for a ride? And we wondered where we'd end up? Well, I figured it all out. This ride is free, my traveling trolls." The only minor hurdle is how we're going to get on the flats, and or boxcars. As I like to say, we'll cross that base one bag at a time.

"Here, take a map." I reached into my backpack and passed out the maps I had copied from off the internet. The maps were of the train routes from Boston to Maine and routes to

New Hampshire and Vermont. I had circled in red our drop off and pick-up spots. It had all seemed sensible to me; Belmont, MA. to White River Junction, VT., then all the way north to Crafstbury, VT. The guys walked in silence as they looked over the maps. I doubted they made sense of the lines and markings.

"Ah, Tags? I don't wanna seem like a dope, but whatta my looking at?"

"You can't figure it out, Lights?" Laughed Capisce.

"Oh, like you can. Go ahead blueberry brain, tell me."

"I'd tell you, but I think Tags wants to be the one since he's the one who printed them. Ain't that right, Tags?"

"Are we really gonna hop on the train?" Paulie walked behind us sporting a slight limp.

"We'll choose one that isn't moving."

"So…where *are* we going?"

Maybe I could've done without the maps. "The train out of Belmont will take us right to White River Junction, that's in Vermont. From there, well, I don't want to say it gets confusing, but, it could get confusing if we don't get off and end up ridin' north…right to New Yawkkk."

"Noooooo, kill me now."

"New Yawk? Are you out-of-your-mind?"

"I gotta agree with Capisce and Paulie, there ain't no way I'm going to Jan-keyville. No way and no way."

I knew that would get there minds off of hopping the flats. "Then study the maps. Four heads are better than one. How'd you guys think we were gonna get to the Spaceman's farm… IF you don't mind me asking? Did you think we were gonna walk two-hundred miles?"

"I don't know what the Beacon brains thought, I knew we were hopping the trains."

"Yeah, how else? I knew, just didn't know exactly."

"Trains, buses, walking, who cares. All I know is all aboard…here we come Spaceman."

Indeed, I thought, all aboard. The early morning was beautiful, but already hot. There was no clouds covering the beating sun. Without the shade the temperature this early felt in the 90's. The flat cars wouldn't give us any protection from the summer sun so a box car would be our priority. The guys walked and studied the maps as I thought if this was really worth the trouble. Trekking all these miles ahead to talk to an old guy who hadn't pitched in like, fifty years? And maybe he won't return with us to talk to Lefty. What then, do we kidnap him? Sure Tags, four eleven year olds are going to duct tape an old man, toss him on a train, and force him to help our beloved Red Sox win a championship. I wish *school* was that easy. We stepped out of the shade and into the sun on our way across Concord Avenue and onto the train tracks. With the extra weight from our backpacks the heat was brutal. We dodged the few cars from both lanes and climbed up the worn dirt path behind the gas station. The walk to this path was slightly longer from our houses but it did avoid Ratso's tunnel, and anyway was better than passing by Ratso's tunnel.

"Lights, just how far out of first place are the Sox this morning?" Lights was our statistics go-to guy. He read everything off the Web and absorbed the numbers like a thirsty towel.

"We're tied with the Orioles, six games out behind the Yanks with fifty-two remaining."

"Yeah, fifty-two games left, plenty of time to fall into last place," added Capisce.

"The Yankees series starts tonight. Have faith. If we can

sweep the weekend series the lead will be down to three games."

"That's if we sweep," added Paulie. "If we lose all three you can toss the baby out with the bath water."

"What the heck does that mean?" Capisce said as he finger flicked Paulie behind the ear.

"Are you trying to kill me today?" Paulie said dodging out of Capisce's way. "Just what it says, whatta ya think? The season is ovahhhh."

"The season wouldn't really be over, because we still play the Yankees four more games to end the season."

"I hope it doesn't come to that," I echoed. "But why do I know it will."

Twotails ran ahead and stood impatiently waiting for us to catch up. When she realized we weren't trying to ditch her she bolted up the path kicking up brown dust. We climbed to the top of the path and now stood beside the railroad tracks where Twotails was a panting ball of dust with wide yellow eyes. I lightly booted her in her behind and she scooted away leaving only a cloud of dust in her place. Through the dust storm the sleek metal rails extended forever to our right then disappeared in the wavering heat. The metal was so shiny and smooth from years of wear that you could see your reflection. Without fail we'd make faces on the gleaming rail then laugh at their circus funny-mirror like reflection. At eleven years old stupid things never really ever got old...until you were thirteen, I heard.

"Hey, do your reflection."

"Ha, look at me."

"Never mind you, look at me. Tags, check it out."

To our left was the bend in the tracks and where we had to walk to wait for the freight trains to slow. On some days the freight cars came to a complete stop, on most days they just slowed. I checked out my reflection. I started to laugh… knockout. "I look like a squashhead." I grabbed the rail and felt a vibration.

"Squashhead. That's a good one. Whatta I look like?"

"Guys grab the rail. You feel anything? "

They all agreed but no one could see any train coming this way. In the oppressive heat the tracks shimmered and wavered making it impossible to tell movement or distance. There were many times when we walked the tracks that a train almost snuck up on us in these same conditions. We had learned that it was a much safer habit to walk off to the side of the tracks where we couldn't get snuck up on.

"We better cross here and now in case it's coming from this way," I pointed to our left and north by the map. "I bet this is the last commuter train going to Boston this morning. Lights, LC time?"

"It is…9:30 on the nose."

"The train's coming from up ahead. It should be the last one to Boston.. The next trains, the next ones, the north bound ones, are what we want."

I looked both ways before crossing (Mom would've been proud but would've grounded me if she knew *what* I was crossing), and waved the guys on to follow. We were soldiers of fortune and I was leading my men into battle…I was a ten-year old Rambo. "Hurry across." Once we were across the tracks an inbound Boston commuter train began to pick up speed and chug past us as we headed to the bend up ahead. The speed of the train was always more intense, more scary that's for sure, when you were up close. By the time the fifth car sped by it was more of a quick blur of silver with red and blue stripes. I held onto my hat hiked up my gear and glanced at my men over my shoulder. The first part of our journey was under way and somehow I felt no fear…just yet. Twotails was up ahead waiting impatiently for us at the railroad bend. In my mind I was the leader of this group, but if Twotails could speak I'm sure she would've told me otherwise.

TEN

We hid in the brush off the side of the tracks as a thirty car freight train pulled slowly up to the loading platform...*and stopped!*

"Alright. Today is our lucky day, boys."

"Told ya everything would be okay, Lights."

"You did not. You were just as..."

"Guys, not now. Grab your stuff we gotta go because it may not be here long. Sorry Twotails, but in you go." I hated to do it but it was the safest move for Twotails, but not necessarily for me. I stuffed my kicking, biting, and scratching cat into the backpack and zipped in her in. She was going to make me pay for this one, for sure. "See the open car second from the end? Let's head for that one."

We broke from the bushes and started back from where we had come. The train had stopped about halfway so we had about one-hundred feet to run and get in before the engine started. We hadn't taken ten steps before I heard the hiss of the brakes being released and the metal slap of the freight cars. We ran faster but our backpacks made the distance seem twice as far as it actually was. I watched the first wheel of our chosen car rotate then stop then roll forward. The train lurched then began to roll. Paulie and Capisce were side by side and about fifty feet from the open car when they heard then saw the train roll forward. Both of them sprinted to the open door and tossed in their backpacks. The train was still in a slow roll when they made the jump up and into the box car.

"C'mon Lights, hurry, toss up your backpack," yelled Paulie.

"Yeah, toss it to Paulie and I'll grab your arm."

Lights swung his backpack up and it landed perfectly at his brother's feet. He took two giant steps grabbed a metal ring on the outside of the freight car then reached for Capisce's hand. Capisce grabbed Lights and pulled him up with so much strength that all I could see from where I was running was the bottom of Lights's shoes above Capisce's head. I could hear Lights's cries of anguish as he flew through the freight car. For a brief moment I half expected to see him lying on the other side of the tracks. If wasn't for the fact that I had to get myself into the now picking-up-steam freight train I would've peed my pants cracking up laughing . I went straight for the spot I figured would be the best angle so I wouldn't have to toss the backpacks far.

I undid the backpack carrying Twotails. "Capisce, Twotails is in here. Catch." I swung it once, twice, and on the third swing Capisce swiped the pack out of my hand. The other pack I threw in then reached up as the train picked up steady speed. I found myself running back to the curve from where I had come. The platform was in the open so it was important I got up and in before the train got there. Trying not to loose my balance on the small rocks and reach the rung before the train picked up more speed *and* beat the curve, all the while my friends yelling, "c'mon, hurry, c'mon,"…well, it wasn't as easy as it looked. If any of you kids at home are watching, don't try this, I'm a trained professional—at least that was what my inside voice was saying. My outside voice was screaming—"Capisce, grab my arm, help, I'm slipping on the rocks." My sneakers were sliding on the rocks and down the slope of the train tracks and I felt as if I was running sideways. Capisce reached out and grabbed my wrist on the rung, which was a good thing because my grip was being pulled in the opposite direction by my slipping-sliding feet. With Capisce's hold on me I got a renewed sense of toughness. With all of my strength I swung my right arm across my chest to Paulie who was being held by the pants by Lights who caught my wrist.

"On three," called out Capisce, "pull him up."

"The heck with 'on three', ya mooks. Pull now," I pleaded.

"One," yelled Capisce.

"Two," yelled Paulie.

"Three," yelled Lights.

Oh, my friends. I'm gonna…I flew up like a bird in flight and landed like a stone on my belly…but at least I landed *in* the freight car. The guys gathered around me to see if I was all right. I looked past them in time to watch the waiting platform go past the open door. The click-clack of the train had nearly reached full speed and I could see the branches of the trees lining the tracks starting to become a blur.

"We made it," I said smiling.

"Yeah, knockout," said Paulie.

"You said it," echoed Capisce.

"Knockout-a-rooney," added Lights.

My friends, if I can't hate them, I thought happily, I was gonna have to at least like them.

ELEVEN

    The four of us sat like seasoned hobos in the corners of the box car and tossed the ball back and forth. After Twotails had yelled at me for confining her in my backpack she went about her business of getting used to her new environment. She was sitting at the open door absorbing the passing air of an otherwise still and sultry day. The temperature outside the box car had increased but it actually didn't feel all that bad where we sat. I'd have to say my idea of finding an enclosed car was an act of a great thinker, and of course able to find one was a bit lucky, too.
    "Here comes my Lefty curve." Lights tried a curve that landed two feet in front of me and to my right but I reached across my body with my glove and snared the ball and tossed it back to Paulie like we were turning a double play.
    "Nice hands. Lozcaino to Wallace to Henry, double play," barked Capisce.
    "When are you gonna get a new glove Tags? That one is all rattied up. Like Ratso Risoli rattied up."

"I dunno Paulie. This one still seems to be working." The glove *had* seen better days. The light tan rawhide and tight web had given way to worn dirty leather and a web I had to constantly mend. (Part of the leather was being held together by wrapping string for presents...my mom's idea). Oh, and never mind the padding. If I caught a fastball in my palm, my hand would go off on a pins and needles vacation. Mom told me to put a pad the ladies use in a girdle or for a girdle, I don't know, in the palm of my glove, but I had to say no to that idea. Could you imagine the razzing I'd take for that one? Maybe I'd start on my dad and angle for a new LC glove this year.

The ball was being tossed around pretty good when I realized the train was slowing. "If I counted right, this is the first station stop...or maybe not. Try to stay away from the open door, we don't want anyone to see us."

"Whatta ya mean Tags, 'or maybe not'?" Lights looked at me and turned his hat around backward and without pausing continued to turn it until the hat was facing forward. This maneuver was Lights's tell sign that he was nervous and didn't like the situation.

"Give me a minute and I'll tell ya. Listen." The guys watched me as I held a finger to my lips for them to be quiet and we waited as the train continued to slow. Without stopping the train rolled past the station and began to pick of speed. "I counted the stops along the route as best I could. There should be thirty-one stops, or, Lights, thirty-one stations. That's what I mean."

"Ya see Lights, Captain Tags has everything in his back pocket." Capisce crawled on his belly and poked his head out the door. "The coast is clear and we're pickin' up speed."

"Hey, I got an idea. Anybody have a pen, or marker, or something?"

BEFORE THEY WERE CHAMPS

Lights offered, "yeah, I think I brought a magic marker."

As Lights searched through his backpack I offered the guys my great thinking man's idea. "Ever time we go through a station we make a line on the wall to keep count. That way we know when we're getting close. Who wants the job?"

"I got, I got it." Lights got up and put a big, black line down the red, rusty wall of the box car—he admired his work "Alright. Knockout. I'm ready for our next stop."

"That probably won't be for fifteen minutes. Whatta ya say we have a little snack?" I opened up my backpack to the guys—onion and garlic chips with a cheese spread. "Let's all pop open a soda, we could use the sugar." We held up our cans and made a toast.

"All for one," said Capisce.

"One for all," echoed the twins.

"Every man for himself." I could never resist a good Three Stooges quote.

"Oh, if our mother's could see us now." Paulie choked down half his soda in one gulp and burped. He looked at me, I looked at Capisce, who looked at Lights, who looked at his brother, who looked back at me…and that's when we lost control. We all burst out laughing sending soda spraying all over the place. If you've ever blown soda out of your nose (and what kid hasn't), then you know how much it burns going out your nostrils. And if you have blown soda out your nose you also know you can't help from choking and coughing. The guys were coughing and laughing and choking and wiping soda off their faces. Twotails wanted in on the party so I made a little soda puddle for her with a side dish of potato chip and cheese spread.

"Hey guys look. Look how elegant Twotails is becoming."

"Whoa, she'll be asking for a bath next."

"Or her own train car to ride in."

"Hey, even her name sounds like a rich cat. *Twooootails*!"

"Maybe she did come from a rich family," I added. "You know the Buchanons up on The Hill? The ones with the eighteen cars and two pools and tennis courts?"

"Yeah, the judge."

"Right Paulie, the judge. Maybe she came from money and is like some kind of anti-establishment cat. You know, down with The Man. Like, 'I'm my own cat and I'm not gonna put up with you money grubbing facist pigs'. I bet that's you, Twotails. I mean, Twooootails."

The guys looked at me blinking in rapid confusion. "What the…what the what?" Capisce took a sip of soda and out-burped Paulie. "What about pigs?"

"That was something my mom and dad said at dinner the other night. People that have a lot of money, ya know…they act like pigs when they eat. They can never have enough food, or like the Buchanons, enough stuff. That doesn't make them bad people, just the kind Twotails doesn't want to hang with. She rather hang with us poor, train-riding hobos on the road to who-knows-land. Am I right you old dirty cat?" As if she knew I was asking her a question that needed an answer, she lifted her face out of the puddle of grape soda (Old Grape Nehi, my favorite) and stuck to her whiskers was a clump of cheese. Even Twotails had slurped the soda too fast and she began to cough and sneeze and snort, which made it seem as if she was nodding her head in agreement.

"Ah-ha, ya see, she would rather hang out with us…us, what ya call us, Tags?"

"Train-riding hobos."

"Yeah, she knows what side her bread's buttered."

"Or all that glitter's is not all gold."

"Nice one Lights. She knows the squeaky wheel gets the grease. You're batting cleanup, Tags."

"Awesome Capisce, I love that one. Okay," I swallowed nervously, all eyes and ears on the big cleanup cliche guy. Here goes, "Twotails is hangin' with us because she knows, she knows we're…she knows we're slicker than snot on a doorknob." I raised my arms in a home run pose. "Oh yeah, baby, major knockout, a grand salami." I started running imaginary bases as the guys razzed me loud.

"Get-outta-town. Lame-o-liscious," boomed Capisce.

"That's barely a single, never mind a walk off homer."

"Bunt single, *at best*," screamed Lights.

"Jealousy, jealousy, they're all jealous, Twotails." I ran by each buddy of mine touching their heads if they were the bases then slid next to Twotails tapping her head. "Safe." She screeched and ran into the far corner of the box car. "Hilbertoooo Ottttoooo," I sang.

"Speakin' of him, what time's the game tonight Lights?"

"7:05 start. I think it's Stevens against Weekley."

"Stevens? Why's Stevens starting the Yankees series and not Lefty? That's stupid. Whatta they tryin' to throw the season? I don't believe it." Capisce threw the ball off the far wall and he caught it on two bounces.

The train began to slow. "I got it, I got it." Lights put a mark next to his first.

"Ya can't start Lefty on four days rest, Capisce," added Paulie.

"I say they should. They need to sweep the series, and you know what they say, 'ya can't win them all unless you win the first.' They lose tonight they'll be…"

"Seven games out," finished Lights.

"Seven out with…"

"Fifty-one remaining."

"I dunno, seems hopeless to me if Lefty doesn't start tonight. Why are we even going to kidnap The Spaceman? Looks like it's going to be too late. We should've done this last month."

"Oh brother, you're starting to sound like Lights, all negative and stuff," I said.

"Hey, I'm not negative. Well, not always."

"And we're *not* gonna kidnap The Spaceman. We're just gonna talk to him and see if he'll help. Imagine if he can straighten out Lefty, get his curve back to what it used to be. That lead could shrink a game a week….and there's what, Lights, how many weeks left? "

"Well, there's fifty-one games remaining, and they play, say, six games a week, six goes into fifty-one…"

"Almost nine times, right?" boosted Paulie.

"Right, genius."

"So you see, there's plenty of time. No need to panic, Capisce, not yet at least."

Capisce tossed the ball to me and I started a toss around to get are minds off the plight of our Red Sox. I really didn't think things were going *that* badly with the team, not as bad as Capisce, or the forever doomsayer Lights. Of course I wanted them to be in first, but even if they were in first the guys and the whole city would be expecting them to fall out of first. Even with the two championships in the early 2000's, the collective souls of Red Sox Nation will never release the many failures of pre and post Red Sox teams.

"Yeah, plenty of time. The season might be finished before I can burp I Kissed Her On The Lips And Left Her Behind For You. This might be the closest we ever get to seeing a championship baseball team. I just don't want to go to sleep when I'm sixty and think we could've done something 'way back when' and didn't. Imagine that?" Capisce caught the ball and released it with some zip on the throw. "Imagine if we're like sixty and never ever saw the Red Sox win it all? What a reverse knockout, a real stinka."

I caught Capisce's fastball in the palm of my glove and my hand went dead on me immediately. I bit my lip and continued the toss.

"Capisce, could you burp a little of that song for us?" Lights covered his mouth and giggled.

"You be careful or I might tie you up and *fart it* in your face instead."

"Oh," we all exclaimed.

"Gross. Don't dare him, he'll do it."

"Ya better believe I'll do it. In fact, I'm *gonna* do it." Capisce got up and started to chase Lights.

"Noooo, nooo, guys stop him. Do something." Lights took off like a rocket in the opposite direction, his hat and glove flying backward. "C'mon guys, this isn't fair. Help me."

Paulie and I were laughing so hard I didn't notice the train was slowing. I wiped the tears from my eyes. "The train's slowing down Lights."

"I think it's stopping." Paulie looked out the open door. "That was quick between…oh geez, there's men with uniforms on the platform. Whatta we do?"

"Quit it for a minute. What kind of uniforms? Are they police?" I pushed my backpack in the corner and scooped up an irritated Twotails. "Guys, move your stuff into the corners and try to be invisible."

"They don't look like cops, more like cable guys."

"Let's hope they are."

Paulie and Lights stood huddled in one corner of the box

car, while Capisce, me and Twotails held our breath in the opposite corner. The train had been barely rolling and now it had come to a full stop, releasing a long exhaustive hiss. The train lurched then settled and stopped...*directly at the loading platform.* It was difficult to tell how many men were out there but it sounded like a hundred or more. I held Twotails firmly as the voices got closer. Paulie and Lights looked nervously at me as if to ask 'whatta we do'?

"Hey Mack, where does this pallet go?" Came the voice from outside our open door

"The open one, number six." Came the response. "And close it up when you're finished."

"You got it."

"You think that's us?" whispered Capisce.

"I hope not." I put my finger to my lips to remind the twins to stay quiet and tried to calm Twotails who hated to be held. "We'll suffocate in here if they close the door."

That annoying beeping sound of a truck backing up was getting louder and louder. There was no doubt in my mind now where box car 'number six' was—we were in it.

TWELVE

The beeping stopped and mens' muffled voices yelled over the idling of what I guessed was a forklift, either that or a bulldozer. My first guess was right, it *was* a forklift. How did I know that, you ask? Because I was brilliant? No, because two long steel forks with a thick wooden pallet piled high with plastic wrapped stuff entered our box car. I held tightly to Twotails and made myself as small as possible in the corner. The forklift dropped the pallet in the middle of the box car and backed out. More voices yelled over the beeping of the forklift right before they were muffled...*by the slamming of the box car's metal door.* We were officially locked in. The voices faded out and the train lurched and we were once again on our merry way—sort of.

"Tags," whispered Lights, "are we locked in?"

"Ya don't have to whisper, pea brain, we're all alone again," snarled Capisce.

"I'll go check," offered Paulie.

"Seems like we might be," I sighed.

Paulie, Capisce, and Lights grabbed the handle of the metal latch and tried to pull it up and over—the latch didn't budge. "Get outta my way, let me try." Capisce pushed us aside and tried muscling it alone. It didn't move an inch. "Must be locked." He pulled one more time then kicked the door.

"What is all this stuff anyway?" The twins were climbing on the pyramid of plastic that sat in the middle of our train car, already forgotten that we were locked in a moving oven like trapped mice.

"Guys, forget that stuff for now. Don't you think we should be paying attention to getting one of these doors open? We haven't tried the other door." I pointed across the box car.

"There's *another* door." Capisce sprinted around the pyramid of stuff but not before giving Lights a quick ear flick on the way past.

"See if there's a latch or a bar you can push on." I forgot I was squeezing Twotails until she hit me with her closed paw on the chin. I dropped her and she joined the climbing twins.

"I think…it looks like boxes of cereal."

"Yeah, Spooky Flakes!" screamed Lights.

"Get-out knockout. They're the best," echoed Capisce.

Spooky Flakes? They *were* the awesomest knockout. Covered in white sugar with all shapes of scary movie monsters. They were every kids most favorite of favorite cereals. I once ate a whole box watching a Sox game and probably could've devoured another if only we had some. This was like dying and going to cereal heaven, which reminded me of the situation.

"Tags, I found the latch," yelled Capisce.

"Pull up on it. Let's hope someone forgot to…" I watched Capisce pull the latch up and slide the heavy metal open like it was the screen door on his mother's porch. Air, albeit hot air, came rushing into the box car; we were back in business.

"There ya go Tags, where back in business."

"I couldn't agree more Mr. Muscles."

Capisce did a muscle pose like the competitive body builders with his arms flexed in front and his neck muscles all tight. "Call me, General Cap. That's gonna be my professional wrestlers name when I grow up. I'll come out to the ring with a long Army coat with all the medals and stars, and a helmet, with five stars pinned to the front. General Cap, ya know, short for Capiscio. Whatta ya think?"

"I like it," said the twins.

"General Cap," I repeated. "One hold from General Cap, and you'll be takin' a permanent dirt nap."

"Knockknockknockout!"

Capisce muscle posed and howled like a wolf. We were all feeling pretty positive and grown up. And why not? On the road by ourselves, more Spooky Flakes than any of us could eat (maybe), and being true grit warriors by trying to help our favorite team win The Championship before it was too late. The guys and me had been on the road less than two hours and already we felt ten years older.

"Hey jerk stack, let's take all the Crazilla monsters out of the boxes and see how many we get."

"Crazilla? He's lame-o. I say we collect Torpedo Tarantula. He's the scariest."

"*You* two are lame-o. Everyone knows Icaberg Iceberg is the *coooolest and scariest*. Am I right Tags, or am I right?" Capisce continued to flex his arms.

Well, we might have felt older, but I didn't say we were necessarily acting older. There would be plenty of time for the acting older part. For know, what the heck? "You three are goobers. Anyone who knows anything about Spooky Flakes knows one-hundred percent the scariest and bestest monster is The Four-Fanged Frog, 'who's able to leap a mile and with blood dripping fangs finishes his foes like a heat seeking missile". I knew the commercial by memory.

"Get outta town. It's Torpedo Tarantula, hands down."

"Icaberg Iceberg, he freezes your insides and you suffocate. And look how ugly he is. No one's scarier."

"Crazilla's *the* ugliest."

"Maybe the ugliest," I added, "but we're talking the scariest. A four-fanged frog who can leap that far and bite your head off? That's got to be the scariest."

And so went the conversation for miles as we continued to count off the train stops. We opened up boxes of cereal and each of us ate mouthfuls of the most delicious sugary monsters that any eleven year old kid could only dream of. Cereal figures were tossed everywhere in the box car but that just added to our independence because we knew we'd never ever in a million years get blamed for the mess or have to clean up after ourselves. It was one of the summer 'no rules' rule. At about the middle of my second box of Spooky Flakes my stomach passed me a note, a reminder, that it still was attached to my mouth, and if I didn't stop eating Spooky Flakes then I would pay in the worst imaginable manner. I closed my eyes, listening to my stomach and the 'thump thump' of track underneath and wondered what the Spaceman was like. He sounded nice in the email, I reminded myself. Willing to listen, I reminded myself. Come on up! I reminded myself, again. My mom would always remind me before I had to take an important test or have to do something she knew made me nervous, "if you pee your pants that's not going to help you not be nervous, you'll still be nervous, but now wet and nervous." In her loving (strange) way she was telling me not to worry. I smiled and realized Mom's words had settled my nerves and my stomach from doing somersaults.

"Hey you bums, who's up for some catch? Lights, you're keeping count, right?"

THIRTEEN

With the boxes piled high in the middle of our box car ballpark the game of throw around was limited to the side of the car closest to the open door. The air was getting hotter so the open door really didn't help, just made us feel like we weren't stuck in a broom closet. We were now traveling through woodlands, outside the city and towns we were familiar. Not that any of us were world travelers but I did know something about places outside my home town, and this certain area I most definitely didn't recognize.

"We're ya think we are, Tags?" Lights was looking out the door and he *wasn't* fidgeting with his hat.

"What time does LC say?"

"It is 11:42...LC time, of course."

I took out my map and checked off the marks Lights had made on the wall. Lights had made nineteen marks. "Well, I figure we're right here." I circled Nashua, New Hampshire.

"Wow, I've never been to New Hampshire before," said Lights.

"Yeah ya have, ya knucklhead. Remember when Aunt Sheila died? That was in New Hampshire."

"That was in New Hampshire? Boy it didn't look like this." Lights looked out the door smiling.

"That's because we drove on the highway. We never got to the woods."

"Let me look at the map while you two girls fight." Capisce grabbed the map and studied it like a teacher would a test paper. "How much longer do ya think when we get to that place if we miss we'll end up in New York?"

"White River Junction? Should be eleven more stops. You never know with the stops, though, how long it will take. Who knew someone was gonna drop off our lunch, right?" I pointed to the cereal that was covering the box car floor. "That reminds me, I'm thirsty. Everyone should drink something, you can get really dehydrated in this heat." My stomach was feeling much better. "Hey, anyone seen Twotails?"

Capisce pointed to the top of the pile of cereal boxes. "Ya couldn't of guessed?"

Twotails sat at the very top of the cereal pyramid licking the sugar off her paws. "Hey, that's the way to get her to clean herself, you cover her with sugar." She looked down at us as squinting, probably wondering why we were all laughing and glaring at her. None of the attention bothered her as she went on licking and enjoying the special treat. I left a pool of water for her and opened up another Nehi. The soda was getting warm because the frozen ice pack had thawed awhile back. I had expected the ice pack to last a little longer but never figured on the heat to climb this fast. The Nehi tasted good even warm as I sat at the open door dangling my legs out the box car. The heat was stifling, probably nearing one-hundred, but it at least was circulating. The guys all grabbed a drink and joined me. Even Twotails forced her way in between me and Paulie and joined in on the hangout. We probably had another hour or more to go before we had to get off the train when a situation popped into my head. It was another 'great thinkers' moment. We passed a pond on the other side of the embankment and for a minute I thought of scrubbing the whole plan and go swimming for the rest of the day, or maybe for the whole weekend. The Red Sox could wait, as in 'wait 'till next year'.

"Look," exclaimed Lights. "Look at the lake. The heck with Spaceman. It's so hot let's go swimming."

"How?" His brother asked.

Ha-ha, exactly. There lies my 'great thinkers' dilemma.

"How what?"

"How do we go swimming while we're sitting on a train going thirty miles an hour? You hidin' a brake you haven't told us about?" Paulie saw my dilemma.

Lights rotated his hat on his head...*twice*. Sheer panic seemed to have set up shop in Lights's soul. "If we can't get off to go swimming, then how are we gonna get off, period?" Lights looked at me, his brother, Capisce, then me again. "No. No way. One of us could die, *or worse*. C'mon Tags, I thought you might of had a plan to get us off the train that didn't include jumping to our death, *or worse*."

Yeah, or worse. The pond was fading off in the distance, just a reminder of how hot the day was becoming. "I had a plan Lights, but when we got locked in that plan went in the dumpster. Now that I think of my plan it really wasn't much of one. I sort of assumed at our last stop we were going to just walk off onto the platform. Not much of a plan, huh?"

"Well Tags. Ya know what happens when you assume?"

Capisce wagged his finger as if scolding me. "You make an ass out of you and me. Get it? An as…"

"Yeah, yeah, I get it." The guys were covering their mouths laughing. Something about swearing when you're a kid made you feel old and young at exactly the same time. It was like a story I overheard my dad telling my mom about the further you get away from high school—fifteen, twenty, thirty years—the more you start acting like a kid again. He called it the 'afraid of getting old syndrome.' Maybe he was right because I walked in one night and they were sitting on the couch tickling each other. I was going to tell them they were a little too old to be acting like that then I remembered the syndrome. Getting old seemed a bit complicated.

"So don't ever assume."

"I assumed once," said Lights laughing. "I ass-umed you, Capisce, were eating blueberries and became the smartest kid in school but at the spelling bee when asked to spell chrysanthemum you couldn't." Lights laughed and hid behind the boxes of cereal expecting Capisce to bite and attack. "And everyone couldn't stop laughing."

"First of all numbskull, it's too hot to chase you. And second, what you're talking about is imagining, not ass-uming. But, you just proved my point. Now who's the one who should be eating blueberries?"

We all shrugged our shoulders and met again at the open door, our attention once again changing direction like a (an old) Lefty curve ball. The skies had turned a nasty gray and black, making the day seem later than it was, which was almost LC time.

"Is it almost time, Lights?" I asked.

Lights looked at his watch and held up his hand with four, three, two, one finger extended…a crack of the bat, a roar of the crowd, and a tiny Louie Cardinale popped out of the home plate at "6" on his watch and ran the bases like he'd hit an inside the park home run then slid into home plate and disappeared. We all did the LC call, "it's twelve o'clock, LC time." None of us ever tired of that. I know we will some day, but today it was still all knockout.

"Tags, tell us the story of the underground tunnels at Fenway Park," Paulie said.

The lightning across the sky was distant but it wasn't long before the rain would be coming. A good rain storm would be a welcome. "Ya, why not? Well, what I heard, years ago, before the Red Sox were winning championships, like around 1990, they closed Fenway Park and built a new ballpark on an Indian reservation. A lot of people said that was very chancy because of the superstitious thing, of course. Here they are, the Red Sox, cursed as it is, without a championship in nearly one-hundred years, and whatta they do? The chaloots moved the park to sacred ground. Bad enough, being cursed, but now the team's got to play on a sacred burial ground? Well, the fans rioted, took to the streets in numbers and actually boycotted the new ball park. Truthfully, most of the fans were too afraid to go, including my dad, your dad, and your dad. The owners were going to tear down the old ballpark but it dawned on them that because the ballpark was the oldest in the country, and it was like a shrine, a cathedral, a place of worship…"

"Amen brother," chimed Capisce.

"Hallelujah," said the twins.

I glanced at the guys as they shared high-fives and knuckle-fists. "You guys finished? Anyway, they figured they'd make the old park like a museum. They had a tram system, which is a streetcar, built under the ballpark where it takes customers on a history tour through the park. I hear it goes behind The Green Monster…"

"No way?"

"Yeah way. That's what I heard, too."

"…cuts under the centerfield wall, ya know, where The Brain is."

"Oh yeah, The Brain. Ya gotta tell us about the The Brain, Tags," said Lights

"I will. The tram continues around the underground and introduces you to life-sized wax statues of the great Red Sox players, the ones in the Red Sox Hall-of-Fame. They move like they're swinging the bat, or fielding a ball. There's something like two-hundred statues. It's knockout. Two years after the team moved the owners realized how bad attendance had become, and how bad the *team* had become. The Sox finished last two years in a row. In fact, more people were going to Old Fenway and taking the tour then going to watch the team play at the Indian Reservation Fenway. It turns out it was a great thing they never tore down the old ballpark. Some people, my dad, your dad, your dad, think it wasn't by accident, that the park was torched by dead spirits, but, be as it may, when the Indian Reservation Fenway burnt down, the team moved back into Fenway Park. The first year they moved back they made the playoffs…"

"Yeah, made the playoffs, only to lose to whom?" Capisce asked sarcastically.

"Jan-keeys, four games to three in the ALCS," said Lights.

"That's right, but not the point. The point is at least they made it *back* to the playoffs. Plus, two years later the so-called Curse was destroyed and for the first time in eighty-six years they won it all. Anyway, the team owners stopped the tram tours during the season, but the tracks and the statues are still there...plus The Brain."

"Ah-ha, The Brain," Paulie said in a scary voice.

"Yes, The Big Bloody Brain," echoed Lights.

"Oh no, not...The...Brain," Capisce said copying Paulie.

"Oh, but yes, The Brain." The lightening and thunder was joined by torrential driving rain. We were getting soaked by the rain which was coming down at us sideways, but no one moved (except Twotails who bolted for the top of the cereal boxes). Instead, we lifted our faces to the cooling water and enjoyed the change. The scene outside our box car if it was in a movie would be considered to corny to believe. We were all making scary voices and talking about a brain, but it was true. The time said lunch time, twelve o'clock, daytime. The outside said dinner time, midnight, lights out. The sky had turned freakishly black, the wind howling and forcing the rain in every direction. At first the rain had been a welcome, now it struck me in the face and arms like bee stings. "I don't know about you guys, but that's startin' to hurt." I backed up and to the cover of the metal wall. The guys followed my lead.

"Well Lights, ya wanted to go swimmin', how's this for gettin' what ya asked for?" Paulie flicked his brother's ear like it was his fault about the downpour. "It's like the end of the world."

"Hey, you guys ever heard that story about the time it rained fish?" I wiped the rain from my burning eyes. My hat had blown off and was being tossed around by the wind. I chased it down and hunkered into the far corner away from the open door.

"Rained fish? Is that why you're the way you are? You got hit in the head by a falling cod fish."

"Good one Capisce."

"I thought so."

"No, really, you guys never heard that? There's also stories of raining frogs, squid, and even cows."

"Get-outta-town. Raining fish, yeah, but cows? C'mon Tags."

"Oh, you believe Tags about the fish, Lights, but you find it hard to believe about raining cows? That makes no sense, no sense at all," Paulie said disgustingly.

"I'm dead serious. As far back as the Bible times there's been stories of stuff falling from the sky. Nobody really knows why but they have guesses. One theory is tornado's. When a tornado comes sweeping past it pulls the water up into its spout and in the water is all the fish, frogs, the tadpoles, and an occasional cow, or two…"

"What, no car, or a fat Mrs. Dashgruber from the school cafeteria?" laughed Capisce.

"Don't laugh…"

"I knew it. *That's* were Mrs. Dashgruber came from, the sky. She fell from a twister."

The guys were yukking it up at my story but most of it was true, except for the baby part. "Once a baby fell out of the sky right into a hay wagon that was being pulled by those religious people that live in Pennsylvania. The family thought it was a sign from heaven, like God tossed the kid to them, so they made the child a king, or something like that. Another theory is the Bible's mention; 'I will plague your country with frogs.' Whatever it is ya got to admit, it's all pretty knockout "

"Geez, if they can plague us with frogs, why can't they plague us with a World Series team, or two?"

"I believe that would be considered a miracle, my son, not a plague." I burst out laughing at my own joke as the guys threw their gloves and hats at me. "Wait, listen." The train's brakes had been applied as we began to slow into the next station. Lights by instinct went to the wall and crossed off one more station. We were getting closer to our last stop.

* * *

"The Brain ruined Major League Baseball," I said.

"That's what our father said," added Paulie.

"My dad said the same thing, except there wasn't any choice. The umpires were so bad for so long, never mind half of them were getting paid to throw the games, the league had to do something. At least that's what he believed, about the umps getting dirty money. Our dads are old, though. They'd rather have crooked umpires instead of computers."

"No, that *is* the truth. The league fired most of them for fixin' games. Major League Baseball had been working on getting computers involved in the game a long time. Maybe it was just coincidence the umpires got caught, but, The Brain was gonna happen anyway."

"I hear it's in dead-away centerfield, right behind Dupree."

"It's right above Stanley 'Porkchop' Dupree."

"How many pork chops *did* he eat that time?" asked Capisce.

"Rumor has it was eight pounds of chops…barbecued," I said.

"Don't ya remember the song?" Lights lowered his voice as best an eleven year-old kid could. "'Barbecued chops, if not made at Burpree Barbecue, ain't got the thumbs-up, from Stanley Dupree.' You guys remember that song? At the end of the song Dupree would be smilin' with his glove on eatin' a huge barbecued pork chop and his face was smothered in barbecue sauce."

We sang the song, off key, like a gaggle of geese with laryngitis, but knuckle-fisted each other as if we ruled the world.

It was Capisce who ruined our good cheer. "That's probably the reason he's hittin' .270…"

".279," mumbled Lights.

"Whatever."

"What's the reason?"

"'Cause he's a fat pork chop. Look at him. You've seen him. It looks like he put on 60 pounds from last year. The porka can't even get around on a fastball this year. I say he's all washed-up"

"Twenty-five homers so far ain't too bad for a washed-up fat porka," added Lights.

"I bet ya he doesn't reach…" Capisce thought for a second, "I bet ya he doesn't hit thirty-five homers. And I bet ya a weeks worth of buying sodas. The guy's all done. In fact, keep an eye on him. Every inning he gains a pound. By the time the season ends he's gonna be six hundred pounds."

"You're gone. Thirty-five home runs? For a week of sodas? Whatta ya think, Tags, should I take the bet?" Lights was rotating his hat non-stop.

"Don't go asking Tags, you decide."

"I say go for it. Either way I'm gettin' a free soda a day for a week," I laughed.

"Wait a minute. You mean the looser buys *everyone* a soda?" swallowed Lights.

"Yeah, sure, why not. Thirty-five home runs, not including playoffs, like that's gonna matter, at the end of the season, or one of us is buying our bum friends free sodas for a week. Oh, and no ties. Ties lose."

"If he ends on thirty-five who loses? One of you guys,

Tags, or Paulie, have to have the final say. One of you guys gotta be the referee."

I volunteered. "Since Capisce was the one who called the bet, and he did say he would *not* hit thirty-five home runs, then the bet should be thirty-four for a win for Capisce, thirty-five or more a win for Lights. That way there's no tie. Sound fair?"

The guys agreed it all sounded fair and square, even-steven, up and up, hunky-dory, okey-dokey, and all the other sayings that meant 'yeah.' We also agreed if the Red Sox stunk (like in *our* lifetime) and didn't make the playoffs at least we had something to root for…well, me and Paulie did.

"Don't forget, Grape Nehi for me," I said.

"Orange for me," added Paulie

"And root beer for me," laughed Capisce.

"Well, when *I* win, it's seven flavors for seven days," finished Lights.

Another stop passed and after Lights marked it off we sat in silence staring out the door at the pouring rain. The lightening and thunder seemed worse, the rain harder, but still I hadn't seen any frogs or other creatures fall from the sky. I was thinking of all the things I wished would fall from the sky when Lights broke my concentration.

"So Tags, how *does* The Brain work?"

All of us at once said, "oh yeah," having forgotten that's what we were discussing before we got the subject of falling animals and babies. "How it works is simple. The batter's box is a computerized strike zone from the letters to the knees of the batter. Of course the strike zone changes depending on the height of the batter. The baseballs have an electronic chip, a sensor, implanted that's like the size of a pinhead. When the ball crosses the plate the computerized zone records where the sensor passed and whether the ball is in or outside the strike zone. The Brain is what makes the strike zone and calls the balls and strikes. They say it's one-hundred percent accurate, never misses a call. I say nothing's one-hundred percent accurate."

"My dad says the same thing, 'nuthin's one-hundred percent accurate,'" added Capisce.

"Boy, I'd love to see The Brain someday. Wouldn't you?"

"Yeah. Maybe someday we can sneak into Fenway and unplug the computer just as Hilberto Otto is at the plate in the bottom of the ninth with the bases loaded and a three-and-two count…"

"Ya can't unplug it, Paulie, it wouldn't record the pitch. You'd have to think of another way to fool it," I said.

"Like move it," smiled Capisce.

"Like move it," I agreed. There were other considerations at the moment, like how we were going to get off this moving train, and how we were going to survive a night in the woods, and how we were going to talk Spaceman into helping the Red Sox. Just a few problems I thought, as I sat listening to the click-clack of the train wheels taking us on the road to an unknown place. Will we be sitting around years from now slapping each other on the backs and sharing an everlasting good memory? Or will we swear, as brothers to never, ever, talk about the nightmarish trip we took in 2023 to the woods of Crafstbury, Vermont? I looked in my friends eyes as they stared out the train's door and hoped I did the right thing.

FOURTEEN

I must of dozed off for a minute because when I opened my eyes Lights was a foot from my face screaming in a quiet voice and rotating his hat.

"Tags, Tags, wake-up. The train's stopped, completely stopped, we stopped…*and there are voices outside the door.*"

"How long have I been sleeping?"

"I dunno. Whatta we do?"

"Did I miss many stops?" The voices *were* getting closer. They seemed to be right outside the locked door, but the rain was coming down pretty hard making it difficult to figure how far they were exactly.

"I don't think you missed any," Lights said nervously. "Well, maybe one, but not two. Definitely not two."

I don't know where we are, I thought. "I don't know where we are," I blurted out in Lights's face. Think, Tags, I thought. The guys need you to stay cool and together. "Did you at least mark off the stops while I might have been sleeping? Grab your stuff guys, just in case."

"In case of what?"

"If they come in that door we gotta go out *that* door," I said pointing at the open door. I reached for a scampering Twotails just as the bolt to the locked door echoed in the box car. As if in slow motion the noise reverberated and pounded my ears like the tick-tick of a clock in an empty room. We all froze for what felt like minutes as metal clanked against metal. Twotails looked at me and blinked and I think that's what snapped me out of my trance. I scooped her as quickly as a cobra and with my bag over one arm my glove on my wrist my hat on backwards and her under another I made a mad dash for the open door. The guys followed my lead. "Don't jump yet. Wait one second." Because the cereal boxes were piled high in the middle of the box car whoever came in wouldn't be able to see us until they climbed up. "Do we have everything?"

"Are we gonna jump Tags?" Lights's hands were full or his hat would've been spinning like a propellor.

"Grab onto the outside rungs. Reach out, you'll feel the ladder on the side."

Lights reached carefully out and found the ladder. "I found it."

"Paulie, there should be one on the other side. You and Capisce grab onto that one. When I say jump, drop your stuff, then I'll pass you Twotails. Wait for my signal…and be quiet." The rain seemed to be coming down the hardest, but at least the thunder and more importantly the lightening had stopped. I took a look at the markings Lights had made on the wall; there were twenty-nine. We were either at our scheduled stop or a few off, depending on how many he missed, or didn't. Twotails started to squirm out of my grasp just as the metal door's rollers made my heart jump out of my throat. The door began to slide open and I didn't hesitate.

"We gotta go, they're coming in." Twotails was impossible to hold. She managed to free herself from my arm and taking our cue walked to the edge of the door and leaped. Capisce missed catching her by a foot as she torpedoed past and ran off to get cover from the rain. This side of the train tracks was woods as far as I could see. Somewhere down track the rails had split leaving these woods in between the other rail. If we had to get off, I thought, which we did, what better place than this...

"Hey, hey! What the...don't *you* move. You're not supposed to be in here. What a dog-gone mess..."

I heard 'mess' said with the kind of anger a father uses if one of his children happens to break a very priceless and very expensive vase that he was constantly being reminded wasn't a toy and to stay away from touching—like the one I broke when I was eight. I glanced over my shoulder and had to agree with the guy, we really had made quite a mess. "Ahh, sorry?" I said before jumping and running into the woods. The railroad guy happened to fire off a dirty word right before I disappeared into the safety of the trees. I stopped behind a tree to look back and to make sure the guy wasn't following. He was standing at the open door with his hands on his hips looking into the box car. He seemed to care less about us than the mess we had left. If he was smart, I thought, he'd close the door and forget the mess. He started to close the door but not before looking for me one last time. I ducked behind a tree counted to ten and peeked out carefully. The box car's door was closed and some of the train's cars were being loaded with boxes.

* * *

"Tags? Where are ya, Tags?" The guys had run in the opposite direction and were down track about thirty yards.

"I'm up here. Walk towards the front of the train." They were by my side in minutes. "Why are you guys going that way? We gotta go north, not south."

"What I tell ya muck heads? I told them we were goin' the wrong way."

"It doesn't matter Capisce. What matters is we didn't get caught. The guy had me in a headlock. I managed to fight him off and slip out of his hold."

"Get-outta-here! He got you in a headlock?" Lights's eyes bugged out of his head.

"No way."

"Headlock? And you got out?"

"Yeah way. And I'm here aren't I? It was close, though." I don't know why I made up the headlock story other than it was really, really fun spooking the guys. "It was so close I could smell the guys breath. And it *stunk*, like cigarettes and beer, and…and…salami and onions."

"Ah, gross."

"How'd you getaway?"

"I slammed down on his toe and when he yelled he let go and I flew out of the door like Superman. I had a moment, though, that I thought I was caught, and I knew I was gonna take the fall for you guys, because I wasn't gonna give you up. We're a band, a band of brothers, and we stick together through thick and thin. Right?" I stuck out my hand and we all punched knuckles, a show of unity. "And if any of us get lost or left behind we don't leave until we're all together. That means Twotails, too. That reminds me, anyone seen her?"

* * *

The sound of trucks backing out echoed around the woods then the train's whistle sounded and began to pull away from the station. We backed up more into the tree covering to be sure we were out of view once the train passed. One guy, the one who had nearly ripped my head off, stood on the platform staring out into the woods.

"He can't see us, can he?"

"I don't think so," I reassured them. "Just be quiet...and don't move."

The guy paced on the platform muttering to himself and glaring in our direction. He obviously was annoyed at something, and my 'great-thinkers' brain would have me guessing it was us for leaving that box car mess.

"Boy, does he look mad," said Paulie.

"Do you think it's because of the cereal all over the place?"

Capisce couldn't hold his laughter. "Yeah, maybe. And the cheese and crackers and soda and whatever Twotails left..."

"Oh, nasty. Ya wonder why. Do you think he has to clean out the box car?"

"Guys, be quiet. He's lookin' right at us." I backed up from the tree I was hiding behind and got ready to run as far and as fast deep into the woods. "If he catches us we could go to jail for trespassing and destroying property and who knows what else they'll get us on." The guys realized I wasn't kidding when they noticed the man pointing and then calling over his shoulder at his buddy. The two men made an agreement of some sort because they nodded, looked in our direction, then *started climbing down the ladder and onto the railroad track.*

"RUN!" I shouldn't have screamed, but, what could I have done...I panicked. My instincts took over and I grabbed what I could and bolted fast and straight through the rain and deeper into the woods. "Don't look back, don't fall. Don't look back, don't fall," I kept repeating, my mantra of survival. My legs were kicking up mud. I was LC beating a throw to first. I was LC legging out a double and turning the corner for third. I was LC motoring toward home plate to beat a throw for an inside the park home…I glanced over my shoulder…

"What the…hey, guys, you can stop running. STOP!" Lights ran by me so fast I almost fell over from the rush of wind. "We're not being chased," I struggled to say between gasps of air. "The guys aren't chasing us. We can stop running." Either Lights didn't hear me over the rain or he couldn't stop his momentum because he never once looked back at me.

"Good idea," Paulie said from behind the tree to my left.

"Geez Paulie, ya scared me half to death. Where'd ya find her?" Paulie had Twotails in a vise grip until he couldn't hold on any longer and she jumped free. "Never mind. We gotta round up Lights and Capisce and figure out where we are and where we going."

"LIGHTS," yelled Paulie as loud as he could. "CAPISCE."

"I could've done that, Paulie." I crouched low and peered back to make double sure the two guys had given up their pursuit. I knew now they hadn't even started to come at us, it was all a scare tactic, a bluff to watch us run away like little girls. Well, bravo, it had worked. "I'm not too sure those guys are gone. Try not to yell just in case."

"Hey, there's Twotails."

Following Twotails soaking wet was Paulie and Capisce, as if the cat was the one who had found them. The two of them, including Twotails, were a sight to behold. Their shirts and faces were covered by bits of leaves and mud. Their sneakers and socks and pants completely soaked and stained. Twotails looked right at home covered up to her belly in mud.

"I hope my glove isn't ruined, it's kinda new." Lights tossed his bag down and began rummaging through.

"A little water's good for it. Which reminds me…" Paulie searched frantically through his bag.

"A little, yeah. This is more like a monsoon."

"Will you two girls stop whining? We got more important things to worry about, like where the heck are we." I looked through my bag for my old leather glove.

Capisce had never taken his glove off from around his wrist and he was now pounding the water out of the mitt. "Now *this* is what you call broken in," he laughed. "Whatta you guys complaining about? All your gloves were in your bags nice and dry. Boo-hoo"

I zipped up my bag to keep everything dry and had a 'great-thinkers' moment. "Guys, grab your stuff, we're going back to the train station."

"Back there?"

"Back there."

"Why? Aren't the men there?"

"Nah, they're gone. Just follow me." The guys slowly grabbed their gear and followed.

* * *

"See, this isn't bad.. We waited out the rain storm for a bit and then hike it north for about an hour and presto-whalla, we're there. Huh, who's the man, who's the man?" We were huddled under the cement overhang that was the platform for getting on and off the train. It probably wasn't the safest of places but it definitely was the driest. "Just remember to look both ways before you exit, ladies and gentlemen," I laughed.

"Hey, this isn't bad. It's like a tree house, except we're on the ground sitting on rocks instead of in a tree sitting on wood, or a rug, like in the one I want to build in my backyard when we get home."

"And you won't get squashed by a train when you walk out the front door," added Paulie.

"I like that, Lights," added Capisce. "A rug in the tree house, nice. Maybe a television…"

"…and a refrigerator," I added.

"Don't forget a stove," joked Paulie.

"Of course, a *stove*. I hadn't considered that, but yeah… with a chimney for when it gets cold."

"We have a lot to build when we get back and *after* we help the Red Sox win the World Series. First we build the field, then the tree house?" asked Lights.

"Why don't we build the field in the morning and the tree house at night?"

"Knockout Capisce. Yeah, why not? I got an idea. Why don't we build a tree house *on* the baseball field?"

"Nah Paulie," I added. "We need to separate our play zone from our relax zone."

"Right. We gotta concentrate on one thing at one time or that one thing won't get done right. At least that's what my mom says."

It looked as if the rain was beginning to let up. "So should we build the tree house in the tree that's right behind home plate in your yard?" I asked.

"That's the one I was thinkin' of. It has the three big branches that go out almost like fingers and a flat part like a palm. It would be bew-ti-ful," laughed Lights.

"A mag-na-feek," added Paulie.

"Ah, we-we we-we," snorted Capisce.

"Don't forget, ah knockout," I said in an exaggerated

French accent. We laughed ourselves quiet and sat peacefully under the cover of the cement overhang. Even Twotails sat motionless, head on paws, staring out at the eerily quiet woods. There was something really knockout about sitting here with my best friends in the whole world planning our future together that had that grown up feel. Every little step we were taking we were somehow growing older and more mature. Then Capisce let go with a fifteen second overdone burp followed up by Lights then Paulie, and well, then me, trying to out do his, and we were once again eleven. Perhaps we were growing older, you can't stop that. But more mature? I'll have to get back to you on that.

FIFTEEN

The lightening and thunder and rain had stopped, replaced by a light mist to keep the air somewhat bearable. The temperature felt as if it had gone up to over one-hundred degrees.

"Does it feel hotter?"

"Guys, are the woods on fire?" asked Paulie.

The woods looked like they were on fire as smoke billowed off the trees, bushes and grass, and filled the air.

"I think it just so hot that the rain is evaporating right off the branches as fast as it lands."

"Thank you Professor Tags."

"You're welcome Capisce. Just make sure you do your homework. Whatta you say we get moving? We should start walking north, that way."

"How far you think we gotta go?"

"I think we only came up short by one stop. That means the next stop is where we have to change tracks. It should be Lebanon."

"Lebanon, yeah right." Paulie let out a snort laugh.

"Not that Lebanon, bean brain. Lebanon, New Hampshire. Actually we have to find West Lebanon. Then we need to hop the train north to Crafstbury, Vermont. Piece-o-pie."

"We gotta get on another train?"

"C'mon Lights. It's like we're seasoned veterans now. We're on we're off we're on we're off we're on…"

"Yeah yeah, I know, we're off." Lights walked ten paces ahead constantly rotating his hat. "I wish we were off for good and swimming and eating. I've never been this hot in my life."

Lights was right. With the rain you'd think the air would be somewhat cooler, but walking down the tracks the temperature *still* felt in the hundreds. I doubted it made much of a difference in the woods, either. We would have some tree shade but the walk would be more difficult around and through the mud. Anyway, we had to stay close to the tracks so we wouldn't get lost.

"How far you think until we reach Lebanon?" Capisce walked beside me in the middle of the tracks.

"Looks like two miles. But I might have some good news." I had been studying the map that I had printed and noticed something I hadn't noticed before only because I hadn't looked for it thinking why would we need it. "There's a bridge about a mile up ahead. Why would there be a bridge?"

Capisce stuck a finger in his ear, cleaned out a mud pie and boringly shrugged .

"I'm thinkin' a river, maybe? There's rivers all over the place on this map. Look, one here, here, here. Why not one here?" I pointed to a spot on the wet map.

Capisce took his finger out of his ear and pointed on the map. "Where? Here?" A black-orange wax-ball stuck to my map where I had placed a black circle. The wax-ball was the size of a golf ball.

"Ahhh Capisce, that's really, really disgusting." I tossed the map hoping the mud/wax golf ball would fall away—I was wrong. The thing hung there like some horrific monster's eye. "You're sick. What is wrong with you? I can't pick that up now."

The twins turned around when they heard Capisce laughing uncontrollably. As Capisce belly laughed the inevitable took place. Noises came out of him from places I couldn't even name. He snorted and huffed and inhaled and exhaled and flailed his arms around like a girl in her summer skirt and then let go with the loudest…well…

I couldn't think of anything else to say, but, "Oh, and one more thing, watch out for falling frogs." What else could I have said?

After twenty minutes of laughing and then arguing over who was going to clean the map Twotails came to the rescue. She walked over to the map and gave us all a 'is *this* what all the fuss is over' look, then she shook her nose over the mud/wax golf ball and…

"No Twotails…*don't eat that*," screamed the twins and me. Capisce had his finger in his other ear and was quietly watching. We covered our eyes as if we were witnessing a murder.

…she flicked the mud/wax golf ball away with her paw like a hockey player would a puck. Again she looked at us with a 'what?' glare and walked confidently past.

"I knew she was a brainiac. She won't even touch Capisce's wax and she eats mice," I howled.

"You better watch it, I got another one…right…here." Capisce pulled his finger from his ear and rushed at me.

"Ahhh!" I screamed and took off up the tracks where the twins had been standing but were now squalling like piglets and running as fast as they could. "Wait up you guys. Capisce, don't forget the map."

I told the twins about the bridge and hopefully, hopefully, about the possibility of water of some kind—a lake, a river, a pond—while we waited for Capisce to stroll up to us. All of us were filthy and soaked with sweat and could think of nothing else but jumping into a cool lake, or river, or pond. Heck, even a puddle might work, clean or dirty. Capisce handed me the 'cleaned' map and walked by slowly. I folded it and stuck it in my backpack. We were feeling the heat big time. Like when Lefty turns one loose under the chin of a Yankee who's hanging over the plate too much; the heat from the fastball could give you sunburn. I lagged dejectedly behind trying to think of something to talk about to lift the guys spirits. We were in a major league funk, a slump of gargantuan proportions. Something that always worked when we're either riding high, or semi-down, is a game of catch. This one game would really have to be a knockout to get us walking straight up and not hunched.

"Hey, we look like a bunch of old men. C'mon. Lights, where's the ball? Let's throw the ball around. It'll get our minds off of...off of..." I couldn't decide which situation bothered me more. The guys lent their opinion.

"The heat."

"My thirst."

"We're lost."

"Don't forget it stopped raining." What little mist that had been falling now stopped. I looked skyward and could only shake my head. "Great. Now what's next?"

"Frogs will fall and smother us," Lights said sarcastically.

"We'll get run over by a train?" Paulie said looking over his shoulder.

"Oh, will you two chowdaheads let up. No frogs are gonna fall. No train is gonna run us over…" Capisce hesitated, "and nobody's lost because Tags knows exactly where we are and where we're going. Am I right Tags, or am I right?"

All three stopped and stared at me like babies waiting for their mother to feed them. Of course I knew where we were (lost) and of course I knew where we were going (not a clue), I probably should say, I thought. But all I could come up with was a 'stall for an answer double question' I like to call it while I searched my brain for something that sounded believable. "Ah, where we are? Or, is it, where *are* we? Where are we going? *Who* are we? Or is it, who *am* I? Excellent questions, even for eleven year olds. We're all looking for ans…"

"Quit it Tags," Lights said nervously.

"C'mon Tags. You do know where we are, right?" echoed his brother.

"I knew we'd get lost, I just knew it."

"I'm just messin' with ya Lights. We're near Lebanon. Matter-of-fact, it's not far from that bridge I told you about. So ya see, we're not lost. You got the ball, Lights?" The truth was that even though I knew we were near Lebanon, the problem was finding the right train north to White River Junction. How hard could that be? I asked myself. Not hard at all, I answered. "Must be the heat."

"What about the heat?" Capisce asked walking beside me.

"I'm answering my own questions in my head." I caught the ball thrown by Lights and flipped it to Capisce to throw back.

"I'm always doing that. It's like 'what color Sox shirt are ya wearing today, Capisce? Do I wear the white or the red, red or the white, Capisce?' You see, it's no big deal. I wouldn't worry too much about that."

"Guys, guys, I think I see the bridge," yelled Paulie.

Couldn't be, I thought. The bridge wouldn't be this close. I hiked up my backpack and started running to catch up to the twins. Capisce lagged behind until even he couldn't bear it then sprinted to join us. We ran full sprint toward the bridge, the heat of the day making it feel as if we were sprinting into a furnace—and the closer we got the more I was sure it *was* a bridge, a high bridge, because on both sides of the track the woods had disappeared. I could see space, open space, from left and right of the train tracks. That could mean only one thing—the coolest, freshest, cleanest (who's kiddin' who, I don't care if it's a waste dump), lake, river, pond, pool, waiting for us only one-hundred yards up ahead. Twotails shot past me like I was standing still. Even she had had enough of this smothering heat.

"Last one in is a Yankee fan," squealed Lights.

Last one in what, I thought. There better be something to be the last one in. Lights slid to a stop always falling on his backside on the rocks that lined the train tracks. Paulie slid and fell beside him. I could only see the backs of their heads. "What is it?" I yelled. "A lake? Is it a pond? No, wait, don't tell me, it's a..." I slipped on the rocks trying to stop and fell next to Paulie. The first thought I had was that the bridge was a lot longer up close and a lot higher from the ground. The second thought was, how knockout. How freakin' frackin' fruken' farfunnuckin' yahoo knockout. I looked up and saw Capisce standing over me with his mouth open. "Don't you dare drool on me."

"Why? Whatta you care, I'll just throw you in the ocean. How awesome knockout is *that*?"

Capisce could not have been more right (not the ocean right). What we were looking down on was spectacular! Somehow the map had left out the wide expanse of the land and the awesome lake that stretched across both ends of the metal bridge. It must've been a mile across. And the water! The water *did* look like ocean blue. Maybe Capisce was somewhat right, I shrugged. If frogs could rain down...

"Incredibly superbly knockout, Capisce. But I don't think it's the ocean," Lights said.

"Who cares if it's water from a sewer pipe. Last one in *is* a Jankey fan. In fact, the number *one* Jankey fan."

"Wait a minute Capisce, Lights, Paulie. We're pretty far up here. We should look...maybe there's a path or something that goes all the way down? Let's split up. Capisce, you and me go this way. Paulie, you and Lights take the other side. If one of us spots an easy way down give a holla."

"I don't believe it. Is that Twotails down there?" Paulie was pointing to the lake and what looked like a fur ball sitting lake side staring in the water. "It is Twotails. How'd she do that? Hey Twotails, how'd ya get down there so fast?" yelled Paulie.

"Right here," called Capisce. "Over here. There's a worn path that looks like it goes through the trees and stuff. Yeah, it does. C'mon, c'mon, I can't wait, I can't wait." Capisce moved down the path as fast as I've ever seen him move. Maybe even faster than the time he had to go into Mr. Sal's backyard to get our ball back and Mr. Sal's dog got loose and chased him around the block for five minutes. Now that I think of it, that day he was just flying. Today he was *really* flying. He called over his shoulder for us to hurry and before I could answer he had disappeared as if the forest had swallowed him whole. I knew he was alright because I could hear him jabbering about 'knockout', and 'last one in', and 'you bunch of pansies'.

"Capisce looks like a black bear rushing through the trees on one of those nature shows. If there is a bear coming up the path I bet Capisce scares the living poop out of it."

"Ah gross," Lights said. "Have ya ever smelled bear poop? I have and it isn't pleasant."

"Pleasant? What poop *is* pleasant?" I said. "And where were you when you smelled bear poop? And why are we even talking about this?"

"Paulie started it," Lights said pushing his brother.

"I did not. All I said was he'd scare it out of him if he ran into a bear."

We started down the path. I could still hear Capisce calling us names. "Okay, I'll bite. Where'd you smell bear poop?"

"He's never smelled bear poop. He's making it all up," smirked Paulie.

"Yeah, I have smelled it. Do you remember that place mom and dad took us that sold jellies and fruits and plants and there was that huge bear in the cage out back? I even remember the bears name, Bear. Don't you remember? Well, I do. And what I remember the most is the bear poop. And I'm tellin' you, it stunk." Lights pinched his nostrils together to emphasize his point.

"You big dodo. You're right about the name, it was Bear. But it wasn't *a* bear, it was one of those big, big dogs. A wolfhound, or something. You always thought that was a bear?" laughed Paulie.

"Yeah, right, and you didn't?"

"Bear, wolf, deer, cow. Did the poop stink?" I asked.

The twins looked at each other and began laughing. "Stink? It *stink, stank, stunk*," they answered as one.

BEFORE THEY WERE CHAMPS

The path was like a snake—weaving around trees and bushes and rocks. The path had been used a lot, the dirt was worn with no grass. I don't know how Capisce made it running without falling head over heels because it was difficult enough just to walk the thing with all the gear we were carrying. The twins walked ahead of me still squawking about bear poop and big dogs and which one was dopier than a baby squirrel... 'You are, no, you are, uh-uh, you are, no way, you are...' That continued for awhile until Capisce yelled from somewhere below that we were 'a bunch of slow-poked looooosers'.

"Alright! He must've made it in," cheered Lights.

"Knockout. Let's go, I'll race ya."

The twins pushed and slammed each other as they took off down the path. Me? I was just too hot and tired to care. Like Michelangelo being harassed by the Pope while painting the Sistine Chapel—"when will it be done?" he was constantly asked. And Michelangelo would reply, "when it's done." When I get there, I thought, I'll get there. The quiet of the woods was soothing. The air even felt less heavy, not cooler, just less heavy. Maybe because I was alone but not far from my friends. A calming separation that in ten minutes will turn into a melee of adolescent arguments. Yeah, that sounded pretty darn knockout if you asked me. I could hear the twins yelling and Capisce warning them. I could hear them all telling me to get my you-know-what-in-gear-and-now, and how I was the number one *Jankee* fan in Boston. "I'm comin'," I said quietly, enjoying the last moments of the peaceful isolation of the woods.

SIXTEEN

"Make way, I'm comin' in." I sprinted out of the woods, dropped my hat and backpack and jumped head first into the water. The water was without a doubt the best thing I had ever felt in my *whole* life. I know that's not saying much, but hey, I'm only eleven. I came up for air and the guys were all staring at me nodding their heads.

"Is this the best, or is this the best?" Capisce was spraying water at me with the palms of his hands.

"It is the knockout best." The idea that a lake's water could make our lives meaningful made me chuckle, but it was the absolute truth, considering the situation. The water was like bath water, but warmed to just the right temperature—not too cold, not too hot.. I already felt cooled and cleaned. I ducked under again, closing my eyes and letting myself float in weightless freedom. All I could think of is how nothing could possibly ruin this incredible moment with my friends for life. I leaped out of the water to…

"*Snakes. Snakes*", screamed Lights.

...watch my friends run past me as fast as they could manage in water. "What? Snake what?" I cleared my eyes of water.

"*Snakes, in the water!*"

"What about...snakes in *this* water?" They were all around us. Well, me. The guys had abandoned me and were climbing out of the water. Now there's one thing other than spiders that I can't stand, and as my luck would have it, that would be snakes. Surrounding me were skinny ones, fat ones, long ones, short ones, big ones, small ones, red ones, green ones, yellow ones, black ones...

"Tags? Run. Get outta there."

Right. Run. Why aren't I running? I should be over there by now watching the snakes standing next to Lights, Paulie and Capisce who were yelling something at me, not in the water *with* the snakes. I turned around to more snakes than there are trees in a forest. I was up to my ears in swimming snakes. I turned back toward the guys and that's when it happened. Bam! Right off my forehead.

"Ya got him," laughed Lights.

"Nice shot," snorted Capisce.

"Dead on," boasted Paulie.

"Ouch," I yelled running toward shore.

"Don't forget my ball."

"Your ball? It's both of ours," Lights reminded Paulie.

The ball floated beside me as I grabbed it and dodged swimming snakes. Every step I took I imagined a snake swimming up my pants or shirt, down my sneakers, or even in my ears. The guys were waving me in like a marathon runner but my sneakers weighed me down so much I felt as if I was running in place. I was only ten feet from shore but it might as well been a million. Move, I yelled in my head. Snakes slithered by my waist. Keep moving, I yelled again. Snakes slithered by my ankles. Don't stop moving, don't stop...I screamed, standing on land twenty feet behind the guys.

"Tags. Tags. You made it. You can stop running," said Capisce.

I held the baseball in my hand, my forehead had a lump on it and was throbbing, and I was breathing so heavy I could have put out a forest fire singlehandedly. But I was out of the water, and thankfully there were no more stinkin' slithery snakes.

"Never knew you were that afraid of snakes," laughed Capisce.

"And you were running away from what? Sharks?" I threw the ball to Capisce. "Who hit me on the head?" I asked rubbing my forehead. The bump was almost as big as the baseball.

"That would be Paulie," offered Lights.

"Yeah? Nice shot, sign him up." The bump was right between my eyes so I felt as if I was looking around a tree stump.

"Where'd all these snakes come from? And what kind are they? They're not poisonous, are they?"

"Man do I hate snakes," I offered. "The heat then the rain must've forced them out."

"I don't think they are poisonous," Lights said. "My science class did a study on venomous and non-venomous snakes, and the ones I saw weren't venomous. But I didn't see all of them."

"Thanks Lights for that *enlightenment* of snakes," I said sarcastically. "If you didn't see them all, then some could be poisonous. What good is that?"

"I think one got in my ear."

"Well, did anyone get bitten?" Lights asked.

We glanced at each other shaking our heads no. "I don't think so…no, not me…maybe I did, but no, I'm wrong."

"Then, whatta we worried about?"

"We should've paid more attention to Twotails. She knew better not to go in the water."

"Snakes or not, I do feel better," I shrugged. "Except for my noggin."

"Sorry about that Tags."

"No way. I'm glad you hit me, I couldn't move. I got this thing about snakes if ya hadn't noticed…and spiders."

"The bump's so big we should name it," laughed Capisce.

"Very funny." I'd have to admit the guys had a point, the thing was a pretty good size bump.

"I know, we'll call it The Tag Stump. You know, like tree stump?" said Paulie.

"Nah. How about, Mount Tag? That's got a ring to it," said Lights.

"That's lame. All ya did was steal my idea and call it a mount instead of a stump," said Paulie.

"They both stink," said Capisce. "I was thinking more of a circus freak name, like, Tags The-Two-Headed Kid. Or, get a load of this one—Tags, the three-eyed monster. We'll paint an eyeball on the bump and join the traveling circus. We'll sell tickets, five bucks to see the monster—you Tags—you'll scare the kids, we'll be millionaires before ya know it."

"And who's gonna be my manager, you? You're all so funny I forgot to laugh. We're not naming my bump because my bump's going away, just like me. We still have to get to White River Junction for the next train north. We still have some miles to go before it gets dark. And we *still* have to find our way and get close to Spaceman's farm. So I'd say we better get moving instead of naming my bump." I still couldn't see around the lump.

"Oh yeah, it's the incredible shrinking human head," boomed Capisce.

"No, no, it's the disappearing noggin," cackled Lights.

"Wait, it's the no more noodle," laughed Paulie.

The guys were passing around high-fives and knuckle punches and laughing so hard that it made me feel better about everything. One half hour ago they were hanging their heads and walking with slumped shoulders. To see them practically dancing with joy made my gigantic lump worth every bit the pain and ache that it is and was going to cost me. Like a great teammate, I thought, I'll take one for the team any day.

"Snake!" I yelled, pointing to a red one that had crawled on shore between the twins and slithered toward the cover of the grass. "See ya boys, it's been fun. I'll be up on the tracks where there ain't no snakes." I grabbed my stuff that had been tossed everywhere and sprinted to the path hoping no snakes were chasing after me. The guys had quit their high-five celebration and scattered like ants to gather their bags before the snakes joined forces and attacked. The tree branches snapped behind me so I knew they weren't too far back.. Twotails was already scooting up the path in front of me as if to say, 'c'mon will ya? Hurry up already, follow me.' Maybe like me she was creeped out by snakes. I wouldn't have blamed her at all. All snakes belonged in cages, behind glass, in zoos, with locked doors, and a moat, a gigantic thousand foot deep moat surrounding the zoo where the snakes are caged. And, as my dad would say, while *they* were at it (I never knew who 'they' were), they might as well put spiders in that moat surrounding zoo. I'd be a happy kid if that ever happened.

My sneakers squished water as I plodded up the path. I

must've soaked up half the lake with them. When I returned home I'd have to put a new pair of sneakers on my wish… "ahhhh," I yelled. I sat down where I stood and violently kicked off my sneakers. With a branch I slowly turned them over one at a time then held them up at arms length. I poked the stick in each sneaker and shook it around…no snakes. The guys were around the bend in the path so I slipped the sneakers on really quick and stood. I'm still gonna need a new pair of LC's brand, Air Cardinale's, I thought—snakes or no snakes.

"Hey Tags, did I hear you yell?"

"No. I mean, yeah, that was me. I thought I saw a deer so I was yelling for you to hurry and check it out. It wasn't, though. Just some chippy mouse, or squirrel."

"Make sure no snakes are following us," kidded Capisce.

Besides all the creepy snakes, the water had felt great and cooled me down. We were all dripping wet which was good because even though it felt cooler in these thick woods once we got back on the steel and open railroad tracks it was going to feel like we were back into the furnace. Capisce had done the smart thing and went right in the water with his Red Sox hat and soaked it good. I wished I had thought of it first, but… hey, I *did* soak my sneakers. Staying wet might keep us cool crossing the open bridge in the sun, then hopefully there would be shade on the other side. Other side?

I hadn't thought of crossing the one track railroad track. Another obstacle to overcome, I guessed. Another 'great thinkers' moment, I hoped.

We climbed to the top of the path and immediately the scorching sun hit us in all its full force. With the rocks and steel and no shade it was like someone had left open a pizza oven door. I ducked back into the shade of the path.

"Guys, let's figure out what we're gonna do in here."

"I didn't think it was possible, but it feels hotter out," said Paulie.

"I bet if you fart you'll explode," snorted Lights.

"Go ahead, try it. I'll put up the sodas for a week," promised Capisce.

"Not now you guys. We gotta figure out a way to get across that bridge, *without getting smushed,*" I emphasized.

"Whatta ya mean, smushed?"

"If you haven't noticed, there's no place to walk on either side of the track." The bridge held one track that crossed the water. "If a train comes there's no way we can get out of the way. Well, there is one." I raised my hand above my head and whistled a bombing sound as I dropped my hand.

"No way. You got me to jump off a train, there's no way I'm jumping off a bridge. How far up is that anyway? Not that it matters, 'cause I ain't jumpin'."

"Looks like a thousand feet to me, Lights."

"Don't worry Lights, I'm not jumping either. Remember the snakes? I'd rather get smushed by a train than jump in a lake with snakes. That's why we gotta figure out a way to get across without having to jump."

"How far across do you think it is?"

"The train wasn't even movin' so stop cry-babying about jumpin' off a train."

"I'm just sayin'…"

"Yeah you're just sayin'…"

"Okay, I have an idea." I had to say something to get them away from bickering or I *was* going to jump into the snake filled water. "This track is for north bound trains only. Which means we only have to worry about trains coming from behind us. Lights, how far down track can you see? A long way, right?"

Lights stood in the middle of the track and shielded his eyes like a scout on patrol. "Wow, the rails are waving like a flag in the breeze. That's weird."

"That's humidity, and maybe some fog. You can see far, right?"

"Looks like it."

"Okay. Paulie, get your stuff, you're going first. Then Capisce, then Lights, then me. It's about one-hundred yards across so I'd get going now, while the coast is clear."

"But what happens if there's a train coming?" Lights was rotating his hat.

"Run like the devil's chasing you" I hiked up my backpack and searched around for Twotails but as usual she was ahead of us and already crossing the bridge. The cat had more smarts than the four of us together. "Lights, get all your stuff together so there's no wasting time." Capisce and Paulie had there gear ready and were discussing what was more knockout, butterscotch or fudge, on their sundaes (not even close, butterscotch ruled), when I turned to tell Lights we weren't going to wait.

"Tags, you hear something?" Lights was still in the middle of the rail and looking intently down the track. "Ha, that's funny. Sounds like a…but I don't see…"

Lights turned his head to look at me and that's when I heard the roar. "Lights," I screamed. "Get off the tracks, Lights, there's a train coming." I bolted out of the shade of the path and ran toward Lights. I could see he was trying to figure out where the sound of a train was coming from if he couldn't see the actual train. Lights turned away from me and shook his head. "I'm telling you Lights, get off NOW!"

"But Tags, I don't see a train…"

At that moment a light broke through the haze that had

covered the train track not twenty-five feet from where Lights stood. Lights froze as I grabbed his back pack and pulled him with all my strength toward me and we tumbled off the rocks and slid into the bushes. A freight train with full throttle open passed us without so much as blowing its whistle. In the thickness of the haze and fog the train conductor never saw Lights standing on the track. The clanking of the train was all I could hear as the guys were pounding Lights and me on the back. It seemed as if the train would go on forever. I looked at Lights and he was mouthing some words.

"What? I can't hear you," I mouthed.

"Blue pails?" he mouthed.

"What about blue pails?" I yelled back as we both lay sprawled in the bushes.

"No. Twotails. He was in the middle of the train track."

"You sure?" I screamed as the last car clanked past. "Are you really positively sure she was on the track, not beside it?"

Lights sadly nodded his head. Capisce had his arm around me and dropped me back to the ground as he and Paulie nearly tackled each other running to the track to see if they could spot her. Lights and I did the same, pushing at each other to reach the track first. Half of me didn't want to see Twotails if, well, you know, the other curious side *had* to. The four of us, out of breath and scared of what we'd see, stood on the train track in the wake of the train's dust, smoke, and fumes, and nervously peered for a glimpse of our lovable, filthy cat.

"Oh no. I see her. Right there. Do ya see her?" Paulie was pointing to what looked like a rug in the middle of the track.

"That's not her, that's a...that's nothin' but a shirt."

"No way. That's a garbage bag."

"Shirt? Garbage bag? Then where is she?" I pushed past my buddies, hiked up my backpack, and slowly started the walk toward Twotails. The haze and dust from the train still hung heavy over the track making it appear as if the track was swaying. Ten steps and I was on the bridge above the snake lake. Once on the bridge I realized it wasn't swaying, it was all just an illusion. The bridge was only wide enough for one train and had no side railings or supports so I promised myself I wouldn't look down at the water. I focused on the "lump" in the middle of the rails to keep my attention from glancing down and suddenly noticed how eerily quiet it was up here—almost deathly quiet. My friends came up behind me in single file and we hesitantly walked closer and closer. Please Twotails, I prayed, don't be smushed, if that could pass as an actual prayer. What would we do if she was smushed? I thought. Toss her in the water? Was that proper? They did that to sailors at sea. We should build her a box and bury her with dignity, I guessed. That would be the right thing to do. But how could we build a box without hammers and…

"*Twotails*," Lights screamed at the top of his lungs almost knocking me off the track and into the snake lake. "I saw her move, she moved, she moved, she's alive."

I don't understand how Lights saw her move before me, since he was ten feet behind me, but I was hoping beyond hope he saw what he thought he saw. My heart skipped a beat as Lights yelled again, but this time…*he was right.*

"You're right Lights, you're right. I saw her move, too," yelled Paulie.

"Will…ya…look…at…that? Knockout. Me too. I saw her move her leg, too."

We all started to jog, then run toward Twotails, until we stood over her sprawled filthy, knotted flea-bitten body. Lights bumped into me, Paulie bumped into Lights then Capisce bumped into him and we all grabbed onto each other so we didn't fall off the track and into the snake lake. Squinting through one eye, I strained to get a glimpse of her bloody, mauled body.

What I saw made me burst out loud in laughter.

"Well, well, well. If I didn't see it myself I'd never have believed it. Twotails is *cleaning* herself," laughed Lights. "Maybe the train knocked some sense into her."

Lights was right. If I hadn't seen this…Twotails was lying on her side looking up at us and lazily licking her front paw. There wasn't a mark on her. Other than her covered with gray/brown dust, she showed no after effects of a train nearly smushing her for good. But how? Capisce and Paulie saw what we were laughing at and joined in.

"How'd she get missed? I mean, how'd the train *miss* her?" Asked Capisce.

We stood over her scratching our heads trying to understand how indeed the train missed as she went on licking herself clean. She could've been on my bed at this very moment licking her paws that's how calm she was acting. I looked up and down the track and that's when a great-thinkers moment struck me.

"Of course," I said picking up Twotails.

"What's of course? Twotails is so fast she can dodge trains?"

The guys moved in and one by one patted Twotails on her head. Each pat released a puff of dust off the cat's head. She was purring so loud it sounded like another train was coming. If I didn't know better I think she was loving all the attention.

"No, I don't think she can dodge trains, Lights. But I do think she can out smart them." I held her up and lightly shook her and a load of dust floated out of her fur.

"I knew it, she can make herself invincible," smiled Lights.

"Knucklehead. That's invisible, not invincible," corrected Paulie.

"Wow. Tags, did you know that?" Capisce looked at me as if I've been holding back secrets all my life. It was a look of distrust.

"Did I know what? That she was invisible?"

"Yeah. How long has she been invisible?" Capisce pointed angrily at Twotails.

"I think you guys have been out in the sun too long. She's not invisible. She's never been invisible. You see her now, right? Anyway, if she was invisible that doesn't mean the train wouldn't of smushed her. It would have meant the train just didn't see her when it smushed her."

"Oh yeah," the guys agreed in unison. "That makes sense."

"I was kinda hoping she could be invisible," said Lights

"Then go ahead genius and tell us, how'd it miss her?"

"Easy. The train went *right* over her." I made a flat motion with the palm of my hand. "See how high the rails are on the track? And see how it's a little lower where the rocks are between the wooden planks? All she had to do was lie down flat on the rocks and the train completely missed her. That's what she did, the smartest cat in the world." I held her up and all the guys started patting her again but her patience was wearing thin and she started to squirm out of my grasp. I placed her down easy and she jumped away like a rabbit toward the other side of the bridge. Which reminded me where we were standing. "Ah, guys? We better make ourselves invisible like right now." We had about one-hundred yards to go for the safety of the woods. I looked down the track from where we came and saw nothing, but that meant nothing in this haze. I started to walk, *really fast*, trying to catch Twotails and most importantly not to trip.

"I still think that would've been awesome knockout if Twotails was invincible," complained Lights.

Paulie knocked Lights on the back of his head with his palm. "It's invisible. Invisible, not invincible. I'm invincible."

"Hey Tags? What's invincible mean?" yelled Lights.

"I'll tell ya on the other side," I said. It was now time to pick up the pace. We had another train to catch, and a spaceman to find. After all, the Red Sox didn't have all season to wait.

SEVENTEEN

"Holy cannoli, Tags. How do we know which train it is?"

"There's gotta be a trillion tracks." Lights was rotating his hat like a merry-go-round. I almost expected him to lift off the ground.

"I'm not sure. Give me a minute." The four of us hid, crouched behind bushes that lined this huge complex of train tracks. There had to be a couple of dozen of tracks that branched off in all directions pointing north, south, east and west. Some tracks had trains on them with no engine, so I eliminated those. There were old, broken down looking engines on others, so I eliminated those. "Lights, you have that compass, right? Can I see it?"

"Yeah, sure. What's up? Oh, I know," he said proudly. "You're figuring out which one goes north."

"Exactly. All we have to do is find which one points north and check it with our map. Shouldn't be too hard." That had made Lights happy because he stopped rotating his baseball hat.

"I wish I had some blueberries," complained Capisce. "A hand full of them and I'd figure out which way to go."

"If we were in Maine you'd have more than ya wanted. They grow wild. I heard they even grow off telephone poles," boasted Paulie.

"No kiddin'. Then what grows wild in Vermont?"

"Apples, apples, apples, and more apples. But I don't think they come out 'till later in the year, though. But you *can* drink maple syrup right out of a faucet on all the trees, ya know?"

"When did you get so smart, Paulie?"

"Guys, take out the maps and see if you can find the one marked, White River Junction to Craftsbury. It's the only one pointing straight north." I found the track on the map then looked for the one that matched it in the train yard. While all the other tracks clustered right then left, one snaked out of the train yard and headed directly north, as it was marked on the map. From were we hid the track looked like a ladder stretching to the skies.

"I think I found the track, Tags. It's that one." Paulie pointed to the one I thought was the right one.

"Yeah, me too. That one."

"We're a team," Capisce said. "Even I agree with you knuckleheads."

"What's the next plan?"

"With those guys working down there we can't just march down. We're gonna have to go back down to the tracks we were on, cross over them, and come around to the other side. Like over there." I pointed to a line of rusty old box cars that stood next to the track we were going to need. "Those old box cars will hide us, give us cover from being seen."

"I'm starvin'," moaned Capisce.

"So what's new? You're always starvin'."

"No. Normally I'm just hungry. Right now I'm starvin'. There's a biiiiig difference."

"Lights, what time is it?"

"1:47, LC time."

"Let's get down there first, to those old box cars. We still have to get to where we're going before nightfall so we can find a place to tent. We'll eat like horses then. Whatta ya say? We'll have this big knockout cookout to celebrate gettin' here."

"With all the fixins'?" pleaded Capisce.

"And then some. We'll cookout and listen to the Sox game against the wusses from New York."

"Sounds knockout to me. Even though I'm starvin' now, but what the hay. I'm in."

"Me too."

"Make that three."

"No, make that four. Okay, this is the plan." So I laid out the plan for the guys, all the while getting them to forget how hot, how hungry, and how lost we could be, or get. All things considered, my hands were really full.

We made it back to the railroad track we came off of, crossed over that and circled to the other side of the train yard. All the passenger trains I figured must've stopped at the last station before here because there was only freight and box cars here. I checked the map again and made doubley sure that this was the right track. I wasn't one-hundred percent positive, but it was too late now to get cold feet and turn back. We climbed up and into the rusted box car and waited for our ride to come by and take us to The Spaceman.

* * * *

"When I tell you to reach up, reach up. You won't have much time," I yelled to Lights. "Let's break up in teams. Me and Lights. Capisce, make sure you and Paulie help each other. I have Twotails." We hadn't waited fifteen minutes when a freight train came slowly rolling into the train yard on the track directly next to where we sat hidden. We hopped out of the box car and around to the rear and waited for the engine to pass. The train was going slow but it didn't seem like it was going to stop.

"It looks like we gotta pick a car now before it's too late, 'çause I don't think it's stopping."

"Tags. What about that one? It's like the one we were just in." Paulie pointed to an open box car about ten cars away.

"Alright. Just like we did this morning. Lights and I will take the first ladder, you guys take the back. You ready?" We all swung our Red Sox hats around backward as a sign we were ready. The box car was almost upon us. "Let's go Lights." I started to jog away from the open box car keeping my eye on how close it was getting. I counted in my head backwards from ten. At one I reached up and grabbed a rung on the ladder and pulled myself up and on. I looked over and Capisce had done the same. "Okay guys, grad mine and Capisce's hand. C'mon Lights." The train had picked up a little momentum, a hint that it was getting ready to speed up and leave the train yard. "Let's go. The train's getting ready to scram." At that warning Lights practically threw himself in the box car. In one athletic move he attached himself to my arm and did a high jump move like an Olympic athlete and barrel rolled right into the box car. I swung my leg up and did the same, making sure I didn't land on Twotails who was stuffed into my backpack. Capisce followed me in. And as if on cue, the train gained speed and left the train yard with a head of steam.

"We're gettin' like really good at this," laughed Capisce.

"Even I'm not minding it too much. I feel like a bank robber in a western," smiled Lights.

"Nice move Lights," I applauded. "Able to leap tall buildings in a single bound."

"Faster than a speeding bullet," added Paulie.

"More powerful than a..." Capisce held his hands out like saying, 'what'?

"LOCOMOTIVE," we screamed in unison.

We sprawled out in the steamy box car and laughed good and out loud for the first time since early morning. Through the stifling heat, nearly getting caught, the torrential rains, the snakes, Lights *and* Twotails almost getting smushed, and us possibly being lost, we still could laugh for no other reason other than we were just too young to know better. Thinking of that made me laugh harder which made the guys ask what was wrong with me.

"I'll...tell...ya...later," I struggled to say.

We settled in, undoing our backpacks and catching our breath. I was still laughing quietly and reaching for something to drink when I noticed Lights looking disgustingly inside his backpack.

"What's the matter Lights, got snakes in there?"

"I wish that was it. Look." Lights tipped his backpack upside down and four flattened boxes of Spooky Flakes came out. Thousands of squished Crazilla monsters, Torpedo Tarantula's, Icaberg Iceberg's, and the bestest, of course, The Four-Fanged Frog. "Oh geez. I must've flattened them out when I rolled into the box car. I was really really *really* lookin' forward to munchin' on them."

Watching Lights standing in a pile of crushed Spooky Flakes almost up to his knees was too much. Even Twotails who sat sprawled at Lights's feet eating the flakes looked like she was laughing.

"Did ya have to take *four* boxes, ya pea brain?" laughed Paulie.

"I took a box for everyone. But seeing I can't give them to you in the box…here, why don't you take some?"

And the food fight was on!

After ten minutes of flying flakes we all sat in opposite corners picking tiny bits of cereal out of our eyes, hair, ears, and even our belly buttons. They were everywhere—on us—and covering the box car…AGAIN!

"Hey guys, if we got caught riding on the train, we'll be known as the Slob Hobo's. Just look at this mess," I said.

"What exactly is a hobo?" Paulie asked as he pulled flakes from his ear.

"Guys who ride the freight trains. Am I right, Tags?" Lights said proudly.

"Yup. But usually they were homeless and used the box car as their home."

"Oh, you mean like Box Car Willie. He was the most famous of hobo's, at least that's what I heard."

"But we're not homeless. Are we?"

We all sort of looked at each other with a, 'I dunno, are we?' look. Technically we weren't, but presently, well, I guess we were.

"I'm getting to like these box cars. Throw a rug down, a few sports posters, a nice TV, and we got ourselves a knockout fort. That's what we should do when we get home," Capisce said excitingly. "Instead of building a tree fort, we should fix up an old broken down box car."

"And where are we gonna find an old broken down box car?"

"I dunno. I haven't figured that out yet."

"I got an idea. Why don't we build the tree house to *look* like an old box car?"

"I gotta say, Lights, that's not a half bad idea," I said.

"What did you do, steal my blueberries when I wasn't watching," Capisce said shaking his head. "Kind of a knockout idea, though, if I don't say so myself. But it was my idea. Don't forget it."

"That's ridiculous. How we gonna make a tree house look like a box car? Put wheels on the bottom? It's still gonna be a tree fort," Paulie said with an air of sarcasm.

"I got an idea," I interrupted. "I'd rather build our baseball field first. After that we can figure out whether to build a box car to look like a tree fort, or a tree house to look like a box car, or box house…oh, I dunno. You got me so confused."

"Hey, I think the heat finally got to Tags."

"I think you're right. Anybody got any cereal?"

And with that the flakes started to fly once again. Once we ran out of flakes we gathered at the open door, hung our legs out, and watched with youthful exuberance at our new world passing by. We were getting close, we felt each other's nervousness, excitement, and anxiousness. This whole trip had been a real knockout, but we still had work to finish.

"So Tags. What kinda guy *is* Spaceman?"

EIGHTEEN

"Tags, tell us the story of the guy who played in the minors who had two heads and four arms," smiled Lights.

Yeah, why not, I thought. It would kill about an hour which was about all we had left on the train ride. Everything on this part of the leg of our trip had gone smoothly. We had breezed past eight stations without stopping, just slowing some, which meant, I think, this trains final stop would and should be *our* final stop. I stuffed the map I was looking over into my backpack like a seasoned traveler, grabbed a very hot Grape Nehi, and joined my friends at the open door.

"Doubleheader McVinty? You want to hear about him, again?" I was excited to tell the tale.

"Ya, you're right. We've heard that hundreds of times."

"No, Capisce. Lights wants to hear the story so I'll tell ya the story. Anyone who doesn't want to hear the story of Doubleheader McVinty can get off the train now. No? Nobody? I thought so."

"Get off the train, ya right," laughed Lights.

"I think Doubleheader rode the train, right?"

"He played when there weren't many airplanes so he had to. All the teams took buses and trains to their games."

"I can't imagine the players sitting in a box car like us going from city to city. I bet their train stopped when they had to get on and off."

"Yeah Lights, their train stopped. You banana head. Whatta ya think the players sat inside a box car? They sat inside train cars that were nicer than your mother's living room. All of them, except for Doubleheader McVinty. Doubleheader had his own box car, a specially made one that was no bigger than a truck. The players for the Boston Red Stockings begged their owner to build him his own box car, even promising to pay for it out of their pockets, if he'd do that one favor. Why didn't they just release him, you ask? One was he was a great, and I mean great, pinch hitter. And two was because the players liked him. They didn't want to be responsible for the poor guy being kicked out of baseball. The players knew if he didn't play baseball he'd probably end up an old man in a traveling circus in a smelly cage behind a curtain under a hot light with kids crying and boys throwing peanuts at him and old ladies fainting and girls scream…"

"Yeah, yeah, scray, scary, we gotta ya, Tags."

"Right. They wanted the owner to build him his own train car because they couldn't trust him. You remember why?"

"Not only was he known as Doubleheader McVinty, but…, drum roll please. He was more famously known as, Manyfingers McVinty," smiled Paulie. "Thank you. Thank you, thank you very much." Paulie stood and bowed.

"What was his lifetime pinch hitting batting average, Lights?"

"Right-handed or left-handed?"

"Both."

"Right-handed he hit .289. Left-handed he hit better, .325, because the head that looked that way was bigger, and had bigger eyes, which meant better eyesight. He hit more homers lefty, too, 26 to 10 righty."

"That's right. He could even steal the catcher's signs which would really drive the catchers' nuts. When he was up at bat one head would be looking at the pitcher while the other head, the one facing in the opposite direction, like he was watching behind himself, would be looking straight but he'd really be peeking at the signs and whispering in the ear of his other head what pitch was coming . Meanwhile the catcher would be putting down all sorts of crazy finger combinations to try to mix up Doubleheader. The only person it mixed up was the pitcher. The other teams' manager would scream at the ump that he was stealin' signs but the ump couldn't do anything about it because Doubleheader's other head would always wear sunglasses. He could never catch him. Plus, sunglasses were allowed, even at night."

"You know what they said? Ya could never sneak up on Doubleheader McV."

"And if you did he'd steal ya deaf, dumb and blind," finished Capisce.

"Which takes me to his manyfingers. Not only did he have two heads, he also had four arms, four hands, and *twenty fingers*."

"Whoa baby. That's a lot of nose-pickin'-house-cleanin'-tools," laughed Paulie.

"It is, or was. But nobody had the guts to say that to him. Lights, why didn't anyone call him names?" I asked.

"Not only was he known as Doubleheader Manyfingers

McVinty. He also was known as Doubleheader Manyfingers Kung Fu McVinty. The guy could fight."

"He was as fast as a cheetah and as strong as a bull. He had arms on him like tree trunks. Well, two of his arms were like tree trunks. The smaller two arms were like branches. But those two arms were like lightening quick. When his strong arms had a hold on you, his quicker, thinner arms would knock you around."

"Like the time his team had that fight against the team from New York. The pitcher beaned him on one of his heads with a pitch and when he tried to charge the mound the catcher took him on. He held the catcher's head in his strong arms and peppered him with punches with his littler arms. No one ever beaned him after that."

"The stronger arms were normal, the smaller arms grew out of his armpits. That's why he could hit better lefty—stronger arms, bigger head, bigger eyes, better eyesight. Right-handed he was a much better bunter. Coming off the bench in a sacrifice situation, Doubleheader Manyfingers Kung Fu McVinty could drop down a bunt on a dime blindfolded in a hurricane."

"Yup, that's what I heard," nodded Paulie.

"Ya still haven't told us why they had no other choice but to give him his own box car, though."

"Manyfingers was a nickname because not only did he have many fingers, he had *many fingers*."

"He was a cleptamologist," smiled Lights.

"Close Lights. He was a kleptomaniac. He thought he was given a gift of twice the number of hands so why not use them. Rumor has it he once stole the umpires watch while he was being called out sliding into home."

"Awesome. Didn't he steal *steal* third base after he got thrown out," laughed Capisce.

"That is true. Story is no one even noticed until there was a 3-2 count on the next batter. The ump held up the game went into the dugout and there was Doubleheader sittin' on the third base bag with this scowl on his face."

"Which one?"

"On both. I dunno, what does it matter. All I know is people were afraid of Doubleheader, not only because he was weird looking, but because he was downright mean. They say he wasn't mean to his teammates only the other team, and the umpires. So here's this ump with his hand out asking nicely for the third base bag and Doubleheader shaking his head and sayin' something about the ump's mother. The ump walks up the dugout stairs to tell the other umpires he's tossed Doubleheader from the game and here comes flying the third base bag like a frisbee and hits the ump square in the back of his head and knocks him face down into the dirt. The league suspended Doubleheader ten games."

"But why did the team make the owner build him his own car?"

"I'm getting to that Paulie. The Red Stockings' players knew there was a problem on a weekend series in Philadelphia. It was right after the ten game suspension and Doubleheader was back traveling with the team. Early in the game one of the players goes down with an injury so Doubleheader's called on to pinch hit. He gets a hit, as usual, scores and is done for the day. Well, he wasn't completely done for the day. He goes back to the clubhouse gets dressed and walks back to the train to wait for the team. When his teammates head back to the train, or to where the train was…*it's gone!* Doubleheader Manyfingers Kung Fu McVinty rumor has it, of course, stole the ultimate—he took the whole train."

"Unreal. Did they ever find the train?"

"Yeah, two years later in some abandoned train yard about ten miles away. All the players stuff had been on the train—their suits, money, and even some of their equipment. The funny, or weird part about the story, though, was everyone figured it was Doubleheader who stole the train. But here he was, standing next to his bewildered teammates and tossing his four arms into the air as if to say 'who would do such a thing?' None of the money or other things that were on the train was found. The owners couldn't accuse Doubleheader because, well, he was with his teammates. The group of players that had returned to the train first said Doubleheader was sitting on the train tracks patiently waiting for his teammates. Anyway, the owners said, how could he steal the train, hide it and all the stuff and get back before everyone else? And not everyone can just drive a train. Impossible, they swore. But still, knowing Doubleheader, not *completely* improbable. So, they did the only thing they could do without singling Doubleheader out as the thief—the owners built a new train, equipped with private locks and keys."

"Wasn't Doubleheader's box car smaller than everyone else's?"

"Right. The owners said pitchers and catchers would bunk together. Outfielders in two others. Infielders the same. Coaches would stay together—and then there was Doubleheader. Being he was the only pinch hitter on the team, he only needed the smaller box car. The truth was no one trusted him enough to bunk with him. Doubleheader probably knew that but what did he care. By stealing the train he had gotten a beautiful, brand new, private box car. Life could not have been better for Doubleheader, even if he had two heads, four arms and twenty fingers."

"Tell the guys the best part," smiled Capisce. "Tell them about his dad."

"About two years after Doubleheader left the team, one of the owners was reading a newspaper story about a train conductor who was famous for taking a train cross country in record time, which had never been done back in the 1800's. What made the conductor more news worthy was his son who used to ride with him…*his two-headed four arm twenty fingered son.*"

"That is knockout."

"Super unreal knockout."

"I would have loved to see the owners faces. 'Hey, did you know, Doubleheader's been driving trains since he was five?' They must've fallen off their chairs."

"I wonder where and how he hid all the money and watches, jewelry, clothes."

"That guy could make things disappear," I said shaking my head in awe.

"Didn't he go into pro fighting after baseball?" asked Capisce.

"Yeah, but it wasn't pro fighting. After all he was through there was only one place he *really* was going to end up. Poor Doubleheader Manyfingers Kung Fu McVinty fought 'till he died at age 52 in a cage with a traveling circus freak show."

"They say he was undefeated," Paulie said proudly.

"He probably stole the underwear right off the guy he was fighting," snorted Lights.

"That's Doubleheader for ya," laughed Capisce.

"Well, ya know what *they* say? Two heads *are* better than one," I added.

"And four arms…"

"And twenty fingers…"

"And who exactly is *they* anyway?"

That question of who 'they' were kept us busy for the remaining of our train ride. No one really knew who 'they' were—we all had an idea, a guess, a thought, even a theory. But when it came down to who 'they' really were, it only mattered to the person who 'they' were talking about. If 'they' said I was a knucklehead, I'd want to know who 'they' were that said those words.

"But if 'they' call you a knucklehead, Lights, not only would I not care, I'd have to agree with what 'they' said," I added as Paulie and Capisce hooted and hollered with agreement.

Lights quietly rotated his hat in slow circles. I put him in a friendly headlock and added a quick knuckle wrap. We were all buddies, buddies for life, and we all knew that. Plus, it said as much in our written blood pact we put together last year. *We* could make fun of each other. *We* could tease each other. *We* could even sock each other in the eye. But if 'they' ever did anything like that we swore on our pin-pricked bloody fingers that we'd stand as one—or fall knocked out together.

NINETEEN

"This is it," I yelled. "This is our stop. Get your stuff. C'mon, c'mon, this is it." The guys, and Twotails, stood ready at the door like paratroopers. I was hoping beyond hope that the train was going to stop—or geez Louise, at least slow a little—but if it didn't we'd have to be ready to leap. The train was traveling at a pretty good clip and as I poked my head out the door and looked forward it seemed as if the trees lining the woods were coming closer. If we waited much longer we'd be jumping into trees. Here if we jumped we'd be jumping into bushes. The train kept chugging along, in fact I think it was picking *up* speed.

"Tags, I think the train is going faster," Capisce said

"It definitely is," added Lights. "I was counting bushes as we passed, and it was like, one…two…three…four. Now it's, one, two, three, four."

"I think I know why," Lights said pointing toward the front of the train. "There's a hill after these woods, I just saw it. And it's a big, *big* hill. Like a mountain."

I looked at the bushes and Lights was right. They started to become a blur. We had no choice but to leap, and to leap soon.

"Okay guys, this is it. We wait another minute I won't have a clue where the train will be taking us. We might end up in New York after all. If we do wait, look, we'll be jumping into trees." I pointed out to the quickly approaching trees. "I dunno about you, but these bushes look a lot softer than those trees."

"Those are two good enough reasons for me to get off—trees and New York," yelled Capisce.

"I don't like the Jan-keys much. So I'm thinkin', I don't like New York too much, either," added Paulie.

"Put me down for a tree hater," screamed Lights.

"Then we jump, on three. Remember, land and roll. Land, and roll." I scooped up Twotails, nodded to my friends, took one quick look toward the front of the train and began the countdown.

"One...two...three." I could hear Lights yelling as we leaped out of the box car, 'what the heck is leap and roll?'

I threw Twotails forward (cats *always* land on their feet) before I hit the ground so I wouldn't land on her when I rolled.. She went flying as if in slow motion—one still, dirty fur ball dropped from outer space. I smiled at her as she flew over the bushes and I readied myself to tuck and roll forward. The bushes caught me like a big cotton ball. Yes, I thought, first part of the plan was genius—a nice soft landing. Second part—finished off by a tuck, one roll, and a perfect T-square-back-hands-out-straight-and-bow. As I sprung out of the bushes and prepared my final roll in my head, something weird, and very, very painful, interfered in my 'great-thinkers' plan—I didn't move an inch. My feet and legs were being held together in a tight vice grip. I bounced, oh, I bounced alright, like I was attached to an elastic band. I went straight up and then my chest and face went into a nosedive...*directly into sticky burrs*! I was going pretty fast when I had hit the bushes that my face and chest didn't get stuck the first time. I bounced off, flew back, and then got tossed forward, landing with a face full of sticky burrs.

"Owwwwwwaaaahhhooohhhh," I heard to my right.

Exactly, I thought, before letting free with my own "yaaaaouchhhhhhhhh," once I stopped bouncing. Sticky burrs were stuck on me EVERYWHERE!

"Oh Tags?" yelled Capisce through clenched teeth.

I pulled a burr out of the corner of my mouth. "Yeah Capisce?"

"I think the trees would've been less painful."

"I gotta agree with Capisce, Tags. I got sticky burrs stuck to my eyelashes. How the heck am I gonna get them off?" whined Lights.

"You must look knockout?"

"Don't make me laugh. Let me get loose and I'll help you." The bushes had to be eight feet tall. We somehow had to free ourselves from our sticky burr prison by climbing *up* and then rolling out. Or by cutting through! Another 'great-thinkers' moment...I think.

"Guys, I just had an idea."

"Tags? I'm really, really stuck in here. I don't think I can move."

"That makes two. My arms get stuck every time I move 'em."

"My hat fell off now my hair is stuck. Anyone see my hat?"

"We'll find ya hat, Lights. Listen. I'm gonna try to cut my way out with my Swiss army knife. In the mean time you guys try to get loose. If I can get out I'll cut you guys loose." I looked through the bushes and Twotails was on her belly lazily watching us as if to say 'another fine mess you've gotten yourselves in.' I couldn't blame her for being disgusted at us, it did seem as if it was one stupid situation after another.

"Cutting through this stuff will take forever with the Swiss."

"Unless you brought your mom's steak knives…"

"I'll shut up. Start cuttin' before the wild animals come out for dinner and smell us," said Capisce.

"What wild animals?"

"Shut up Capisce," I said. Yeah, what wild animals? I thought. My Swiss knife was thankfully in the pocket of my pants. On the Swiss was a small pair of scissors along with a saw that I knew I'd never once sharpened. I unhinged the scissors, flipping them over in my right hand and manipulating them like it was my first time using them—I didn't have a clue how to use them. But scissors are scissors, and if they're sharp? I held my breath that they were because the saw looked rusty. I reached out slowly and snipped—the scissors cut the thin branch like it was butter.

'Hey, will ya look at that. Cuts through like a butter knife in butter. I'll have ya out before you can say 'Lights likes lemon lollipop lunches while laying in lilac lilies.'"

Yeah, I know, it was a little lame-o, but I made it up on the spot. Another GREAT-THINKER moment! While the guys fumbled over the tongue twister—you should've heard them with the sticky burrs in their mouths—I methodically, and not too slowly, cut myself free of my sticky burr prison. I pulled myself free and took a deep breath of still, sweltering, hot air. But man did it feel good.

"Wow, you guys *are* stuck." That was an understatement. Lights looked like he was the volunteer for a knife thrower in a circus—his legs and arms were pinned out to his sides and he was sort of standing sideways. Paulie was, well, standing *on* his head. "How did you do that?" I looked at him upside down. Capisce had tried to bull his way free and had nearly accomplished it if it wasn't for the vine that had wrapped itself around his ankle keeping him from reaching down and untangling it. The poor guys looked like sad prisoners behind bars waiting to get rescued, or at least fed.

"Sorry if I laugh, guys. But you should see yourselves."

"Tags, I swear…if I get out of here on my own you better hope…"

I held my breath so as not to laugh. "I'm sorry. I know it's not funny. Why don't I get you out first, Capisce. Then you can help me get them out." I know what's better sometimes.

Twenty minutes later we were all standing outside of the nasty sticky burr bushes wondering at our stupidity and picking burrs off each other like animals in the wild. Other than having *a lot* of scratches, we were none the worst for wear. I even thought of bringing along a first aid kit so I was able to pass out an antibiotic and plenty of band-aids for our many scratches. If someone saw us they'd have to say the bushes got the best of us…in spades!

"All we need is a fife and drum and a flag and we limp onto Spaceman's farm. How could he ever refuse to help us?" I asked.

"We should find some berries and smudge it all over our faces to make it look like blood."

"Knockout Paulie. Yeah, some raspberries. I like it."

"What's a fife?" asked Lights.

"I'll take this one," boasted Capisce. "Remember, *I'm* the one that's been eating blueberries. It's a flute."

"Then why don't you say flute and drum. Nobody knows what a fife is. Everyone knows a flute."

"'Cause that's what they called them then," Capisce said impatiently.

"Who's they? And when's then?"

Here we go again with 'they,' I thought while looking at the map. It was nearing the moment when I had to interrupt the silliness and get the guys moving.

"'Then' is the Civil War. 'They' are the Civil War people. And if you were listening Lights, I said it was *like* a flute. Well, it is a flute, but more like a piccolo—but louder."

"You never said 'like.'"

"Drop it Lights," pleaded his brother. "Piccolo, flute, fife, who cares? Let's get going before we get eaten alive out here."

"Hey Capisce, say pee-colo again. Pee-colo," repeated Lights.

"Oh yeah...and I did say 'like.'"

I folded the map and put it away and was about to point toward the direction we had to go when Lights flew past me with Capisce following.

If I wasn't hot and tired and sore I'd have laughed, but I just shook my head and waved my hand. "That's it guys, you're heading in the right direction."

"Do ya think he'll catch him?" asked Paulie jokingly.

"Oh yeah. I just wonder if it's gonna be knuckle twisters, nuggies, or finger snaps to the ears." Just then Lights was tackled by Capisce.

"Looks like twisters *and* nuggies."

"Ouch. Capisce's twisters are nasty."

We walked in silence, past a pleading Lights who was begging "uncle," and through the woods of what I thought—but hoped more—was the last part of our trip. Just out of these woods was an open farm—that was where we'd be camping out tonight. Even though my legs felt heavy, thinking of how far we'd come and how close we were of actually meeting the Spaceman gave me an energy boast. I hiked up my backpack and took longer strides. Keep your eyes on the prize, my father used to say. That's right Dad, I thought, you forget why then you forget how. Paulie sided up to me, followed by Capisce, Twotails (I put a band aid on her butt), and a completely out of breath Lights—he was rubbing his arm, his head, *and* his ear.

"What's…the…hurry?"

Capisce, Paulie, and I, broke into hysterical laughter as we marched through the woods and across the open field.

"What? What I say? What's so funny? C'mon guys. You guys stink."

No one really knew why we were laughing out of control, and for the best, no one really cared. I walked next to Lights and tossed an arm around his neck. I gave him a tight squeeze and left his side walking faster. The guys caught up, Twotails shot past us, and on we trekked, four kids covered in antibiotic and band aides determined to right a sinking Red Sox ship no matter the consequences.

TWENTY

I raised my arm to halt my troops—I have to admit I've been watching way too much of the History Channel—as if we'd come to our final destination. I unfolded my map, looked down, looked up, looked around, and emphatically pointed to a marking on the map.

"Unpack guys…we're here!"

"Yahooo. Knockout."

"We made it? I mean, we *made* it."

"Yeah Lights. We really did make it."

"Now, if we had cell phones we could call Spaceman and tell him we're here."

"You know the rules, not 'till we're thirteen. How dumb can you get? Stupid rules…"

"Parents can't be parents without *some* rules, Paulie. No matter how unknockout," I added.

"I suppose. How 'bout that, Twotails," Paulie twirled the cat in circles, already forgetting 'stupid rules.' "We made it to…

to. Where'd we make it to again, Tags?" Paulie put Twotails down and she took one step and fell over from being dizzy.

"We're near the place we're gonna meet Spaceman tomorrow. We're in White River Junction. Guys, we actually made it, on a train, *alone*, like hobos, from Belmont to Vermont. Do you know how awesomely knockout that is? We're like pioneers, famous explorers. Our names will be remembered like, Ponce de Leon, Magellan, Columbus, Vespucci, Sir Walter Raleigh..."

"Oh, my dad loves that guys pipe tobacco," uttered Lights.

"What's ya dad, like fifty? Who smokes pipes anymore anyway?" snickered Capisce.

"My dad...and Sir Walter Raleigh."

I dropped my backpack and looked helplessly at my friends. "Please tell me when we're say, thirty, some of us will have gotten smarter? That's all I ask."

"Nooooo problem here."

"I'm smarter everyday. In fact, I can feel my brain growing as I talk."

"That's cobwebs you here when the wind blows through your ears. Anyway, like I told ya, I eat blueberries by the bushel, and if I keep eating them...by the time I'm thirty I'll be a genius."

"Or completely blue like the Smurfs."

"Okay guys, we tent here for the night." For the next hour we tripped over, wrestled with, cussed at, got tied up in and nearly gave up on, the setting of our tent. We all knew what we were doing better than the other guy, but in the end we managed to accomplish what should've been a "simple task," as it said in the directions.

"It's crooked," said Lights.

"It's up," said Paulie.

I stood back with the guys and admired our work. Lights was right, but so was his brother. It was the best looking crooked tent on an open field in White River Junction, Vermont, *I've* ever seen.

"Should we straighten it out?"

"Did they straighten out the leaning Tower of Pizza? No. Do you know why? Because it's got class. Our tent has class." Capisce stood in front of us and put out his fist. "I say we leave the tent…we leave the tent…tilted. Who's with me? The tilted tent of White River Junction."

"Keep eating those blueberries Capisce." I pushed my fist in the circle.

"It is kinda classy, in a really weird way. But, leave it tilted the people cried." Paulie punched in.

"Okay. But I'm sleepin' on the high end." Lights picked up Twotails and together the five of us punched fists, once again unified.

* * *

"Our parents were talking about moving next year. Maybe to Florida," said Lights.

"Yeah. On account of some job promotion. Whatever the reason it is so not knockout," finished Paulie.

"When were you guys gonna tell us?" I had just finished cooking us some bacon and eggs that miraculously hadn't been smashed through our travels—well, mine hadn't. Lights and Paulie's had broken and made a mess in their overnight bags. Capisce just didn't bring any eggs, but he did bring bacon. We were lying on our sleeping bags around the stove enjoying the food and the cooling early evening air. "Your parents can't move to Florida. We made a pact, remember?

We were always gonna hang out together. Work together, get an apartment together. Yeah, this definitely is not knockout."

"You guys move to Florida and who ya gonna root for? Florida's baseball team sucks eggs," burped Capisce.

"I guess we'd still root for the Red Sox. I dunno, you're right, it won't be the same."

The air had turned cooler, the sky orange and red. Paulie had fiddled with the radio enough and finally had pulled in a faint reception of the Red Sox game. Downtown Davey Higgins was reading the starting lineups and I smiled inside. Lying around on a beautiful summer night listening to the baseball game on the radio with my best friends in the entire universe gave me that comforting feeling that settles in your soul. You wish you could save it there forever—like a bug in a jar. I passed out drinks for everyone as Downtown read the lineups and I settled back on top of my sleeping bag to count the stars that were now forming in the sky.

"Guys, if you make your eyes cross-eyed it's easier to find the stars. It also looks like there's a gazillion billion zillion stars up there."

"Oh, wow."

"Seems like you can reach up and touch them they're so close."

"Ten bucks to the first one who finds the Little Dipper," said Lights.

"Dipper. I love that word," snickered Capisce.

"You're on Lights. Ya better have the ten bucks on you 'cause I'm the star finding king."

So the Beacon's might move, I thought sadly as I searched the sky for the Little Dipper. Maybe that's it. Maybe the stars above are like your friends—some shine brightly, some faintly, and then some just go dark and fade out. There's no way of telling which ones will continue on. Perhaps the star I'm staring at now will twinkle then die. Or maybe it will continue to burn bright thousands of years after I'm gone. If the Beacon's move I know I'll probably never see them again. It doesn't mean, though, the star isn't burning brightly somewhere, it just means I have to scrunch up my face and look cross-eyed to find them.

"*Shooting star, shooting star*! I just saw a...oh, there's another, and another!" screamed Lights.

"Hurry up and make a wish."

I wished my friends would never move. I wished the Red Sox would win the World Series *every* year. And I wished I'd stay a kid forever.

"Do you want to know what I wished for?" asked Lights.

"Ya can't tell us. If you do it won't happen."

"It's not like I'm wishing for a million bucks. It's just, well, it's just I wish we stay friends forever. Even if we do move to stupid Florida."

"There ya go Lights, you just punched your ticket to stupid Florida," grumbled Capisce. "Ya better pick another shooting star to wish upon. And when you do wish we stay friends forever, *don't tell me.*"

We were stretched out on our sleeping bags weary from our trip. As each minute passed and the sky darkened the stars would magically appear and one of us would point and proclaim "I see one," as if he was the conqueror star gazer. I'd never seen so many stars before—it was if there was more star in the sky than sky in the sky. As I watched the stars fly past, Twotails stalked unseen bugs to me in the short grass like a seasoned hunter. She pounced and pounced and pounced as Downtown Davey Higgins called strike three on Red Sox slugger Tony Pelagrini.

"Yankees are coming up. C'mon Lefty, we need this game," pleaded Lights.

Lights was right. This series in Yankee Stadium meant the whole season—in our minds, at least.

"Lights, remind me again. How many games left in the year?" I asked.

"Fifty-two left and we're six games out. We gotta sweep this series, there's no other way…"

"How are they gonna sweep the Yanks *in* Yankee Stadium? We got a better chance in seeing a flying saucer."

"Look! A flying saucer!" I yelled.

"The Sox have a chance. If Lefty wins tonight, then Franklin—who's been pitching a lot better the second half—can pick one up, then the lead's down to four. They can do it, I know they can do."

Capisce who was stretched out on top of his sleeping bag raised his head off his arms and looked over at me with a puzzled look. I knew exactly what he was thinking. Even Paulie looked at both of us with a quizzical expression.

"What'd you do, Lights, fall on your head when you jumped off the train? What's with the positive attitude? You're never positive," asked Capisce.

"Starting today, right now, I'm gonna be Mr. Positive. No more negative. Just you guys watch. The Red Sox will sweep the Jan-keys plow through the rest of the season and sweep the playoffs on the way to another World Championship. How's that for major positive?"

"Another World Championship? How about winning one while I'm alive."

"Then why are we here? We got Mr. Positive with us—we don't even have to ask Spaceman for help. All the Red Sox need is Lights being positive. Why didn't we think of that, oh,

BEFORE THEY WERE CHAMPS

I dunno, in April when the season started? The Sox could've been undefeated. I hold you responsible Lights."

"Yeah, right Capisce. It's all my fault. You know, you guys could've been more positive, too. You should all have more positive chi."

"Whoa, whoa, whoa. Positive what? Chi? What the heck is chi?" snorted Paulie.

"Boy, you guys don't know anything. Chi is energy. It's when…"

"Guys shut-up for a second. What in the world…is…*that*?"

As Downtown Davey Higgins was calling a static filled strikeout by Lefty Van Heller, Capisce was nervously pointing to something that was standing in the grass about twenty feet away. The "thing" was standing rock still on two legs and staring at us with two of the most angriest, blood red eyes I've *ever* seen. It stood about five feet tall with a round belly and long thick baseball bat legs. It was bald with a neck like a weightlifter. On the back end of this thing was this huge fan-shaped feathered tail that looked like a weathered brown sail off a boat. Its beak was curved like a butchers knife—in and out darted this yellow tongue like it had just located its dinner. I looked at the guys and tried to decide, if I was this thing, which one of us would I eat first.

"Oh my God, it's a gila taranazauras," whispered Lights. "He thinks we're his dinner."

"A gila-what? It looks like a bird of some kind."

"Right. That's what a gila taranazauras is, Paulie."

Twotails had stopped pouncing and was now hiding in the grass behind me. I couldn't say I blamed her—she probably looked like an appetizer to this gila whatever. Curiously, part of me wanted to drop everything and run in the other direction, but another part wanted to attack and chase toward it.

"Does everybody have their flashlights?" I quietly asked. I was having another great-thinkers moment—I think.

Its mouth opened wide then closed slowly. I swore I saw large fangs dripping with fresh meat and blood. No sound came out of the monster, it just opened and closed its beak like it was trying to scare us.

"Yeah. What exactly are you plannin', Tags?" They held their flashlights up for me to see.

"When I count to three we're gonna shine our flashlights in the monster's eyes."

"What's that gonna do?" whispered Li;ghts.

"Beats me, but I can't stand that thing staring at us like that."

"I don't mind it staring, it's kinda cute."

"Cute? Looks like Crazilla from the Spooky Flakes."

"Okay, here goes. One…two…three." The beams of our four flashlights hit the monster square in the eyes—I'd have to say it was a zillion to one shot. The monster's red eyes spread wide, its mouth opened, and the loudest, shrillest yelp blared from out of the monster's mouth—the screech sounded like a dog that got his tail run over. The monster turned and ran—and I did the most foolish thing in the whole, wide world. No, make that the whole, wide *universe*.

"Lets get it!" I screamed. I scooped Twotails and tossed her kicking and scratching into the tent.

I zipped her in, and with flashlight in hand, took off after the screeching monster. The guys were standing watching me as I zipped the tent but no one had said a word—I think they honestly didn't believe I was going to chase the thing.

"Tags, the thing wants to eat us. Why do we want to chase it?" Lights was spinning his cap on his head.

"I'll go," said Capisce.

"It's not gonna be able to eat all four of us. Maybe just one, but not four. I'm only kiddin' Lights." I could sense Lights had lost his sense of humor. "Why don't you stay here and guard the tent Lights."

"C'mon guys, it's gettin' away."

Lights looked around then grabbed his flashlight. "No, on second thought, I'm coming. I'm not stayin' here alone."

"All right! The team is together. Pack up guys, let's get… *Crazilla*," yelled Capisce.

We chased out of the field and into the woods with our flashlights leading the way. The monster had a bit of a start on us but instead of running on a straight path the thing was darting left and right, zig—zagging around trees and quite honestly making me dizzy. With all its running it was only about fifteen yards up ahead.

"Hey, will ya look at that? The thing runs like Capisce runs the bases."

"Keep your flashlights on it."

"Where'd it go? Oh, I got it. It sounds like a screaming kitten."

"I lost it," I yelled. We were spread out in a line about ten feet apart and running farther and farther into the woods. The whole idea to go chasing into the dark woods hadn't quite hit me yet as being idiotic—I'd have to think not one of my brightest great-thinkers moment—but it was quickly becoming darn right foolish. The early evening had become night as if a light switch had been flipped off. I sprayed my flashlight beam ahead, but now I wasn't looking for "Crazilla," now I was trying not to trip over any fallen trees, branches, or anything dead in the woods. We kept running, though, not sure of what direction we were heading. I knew each one of us was thinking the same thought—I'm not going to be the first one who wimps out and stops.

"Does anyone see it?" yelled Paulie.

"I'm right on its tail," screamed Lights.

Lights? I thought disbelievingly. I could hear Capisce rooting him on like a hitter at the plate. 'Go get ém kid,' and 'you can do it Lights.' It then occurred to me if we did corner "Crazilla" what were we going to do with it anyway? Were we going to bring it home? Maybe cook it and eat it? I know, make it our pet.

"Hey Tags? Maybe it's a good idea if we…"

It was the cannon shot that exploded over our heads that stopped Paulie in mid-sentence and us in our tracks. I looked quickly to my right to call out their names and didn't see the tree limb that had fallen in my path. I tripped over it going full speed and fell face first into a tree the size of a house—my nose blocked my fall. More stars that were above me in the night sky were now dancing in my head. And I never would have believed that old tale, but I could *actually hear* the tweeting of a pretty little yellow canary in my ears.

"Tags? Tags? Ya gotta get up we gotta get outta here we gotta hurry."

"C'mon c'mon c'mon. They're comin' they got guns and machine guns and cannons and…oh geez, look at all the blood."

I had a million and one questions but I didn't know where to begin. First one would've been, "what blood?" Then I put my hand on my face and held my fingers in Capisce's flashlight beam—just like that the pretty little yellow canary stopped tweeting. I found my flashlight and with Capisce and Paulie by my side we made a bee line back (hopefully) toward our tent.

"What was that explosion?" I managed to blurt while trying to breath through my mouth.

"Ya mean the gunshot?" asked Paulie.

"Yeah the gunshot, whatta you think he meant?" yelled Capisce. "Somebody was shooting at us."

I tried to guide us straight through the woods like we had come, by memory, but it had gotten so dark that at this point I was guessing and hoping on all the shooting stars that this was the correct way. We weren't about to stop, though, so we kept running our flashlights guiding the way.

"Why would somebody shoot at us? We didn't do anything."

"Maybe they were shooting at that thing."

"Or maybe we were gonna see something we shouldn't be seeing?"

"Like a murder. Yeah, that's where the Mafia buries bodies...in the woods."

"Oh, I saw this movie and in it these guys found a plane wreck in the woods and when they went through the wreck they found these bags of money, like over a million bucks worth. So they took the bags with all the money and buried them and waited until all the cops left—maybe these guys were burying money and we came on them unexpectedly."

While Capisce and Paulie tried to out do each other on who was shooting at us—if anyone was actually shooting at us—I realized we had come to the edge of the woods. We stumbled out of the woods and when our sneakers hit the grass it was like we were rounding third base and heading for home. The guys were running on either side of me, and the moment we came out of the woods both of them, without knowing the other one had done the same, reached out and grabbed my shoulder to propel themselves forward. The race was on.

We ran hard and as long as our legs and lungs could take

us, bumping and grabbing each other through the grass with only our flashlights to lead the way—there was no way I was going to allow them to get there first. I stumbled once, tripped almost, and nearly fell. I grabbed Capisce's arm to right myself and lunged—I was the first to reach our tent. I blurted out triumphantly with burning lungs, "we're…safe now…here…we…made it," as if a vinyl tent would protect us from the evils of the night bearing down on us. We tore through the opening of our impenetrable fortress and zipped us in and "them" out. Twotails hissed and jumped back not expecting our forced entry. We collapsed, breathing heavily but attempting to be quiet so as not to give away our secure place.

"Shut off the flashlights," I huffed, wiping blood off my face.

"Yeah, yeah," whispered Paulie.

"Hurry," croaked Capisce.

We sat in silence catching our breath. I slowly clicked on my flashlight and pointed the beam of light at Paulie, then Capisce, then back in Paulie's eyes. "Where's your brother?"

"My brother?"

"Yeah, your brother. Where's Lights?"

"I thought he was with you, I mean, in front of you."

"Don't look at me," added Capisce. "I thought he was in front of you."

I shut the flashlight off, afraid to move or speak. I could feel the guys eyes on me asking, "whatta we do now?"

We had lost Lights in the middle of the Vermont woods… with forest beasts breathing down his neck.

TWENTY-ONE

"How in the…how'd we lose Lights?"

"We didn't lose him, maybe he lost us," boasted Capisce.

"You were the closest to him, Capisce. You could've reached out and…"

"No, no, I was chasin' him. He was like twenty feet…"

"Enough you two. What does it matter now who was the closest? What matters is Lights is alone out there with a gang of murderers, or Mafia, or plane robbers, or whatever other creeps you two can come up with, and he needs our help. We're not helping him sittin' in here blaming each other."

"What if they shot him? I'll have to run away from home because my mother will kill me."

"We'll leave the tent up, you can live here. We'll come visit you and bring you food and tell you how the Sox are doing. Won't we Tags?"

"C'mon, we gotta go find him." I unzipped the tent flap and stepped out and came face to face with another flashlight beam. The light from this flashlight blinded me and I couldn't see past it. It was like those big spotlights from the prisons that catch escape convicts. "What the…"

"Tags, Paulie, Capisce—look who I found? Or should I say, look who found me…us?"

"Lights? Alright, you're alright," yelled Paulie.

"We were just comin' to save your skin."

"Save my skin? Nah, I'm okay. Spaceman here knows his way around pretty good—seeing it's his farm we're on. It's a good thing he didn't shoot us, well, he could've if he wanted to but he didn't. He didn't, right? Nah, he didn't shoot you. He just shot in the air to scare the wild turkey off. Ain't that right Spaceman?"

We stood there like three cement heads listening to Lights run his mouth when it finally occurred to me that standing next to Lights with one hand full of Lights's shirt collar and the other hand holding the biggest gun I've ever seen, was a mountain of a man with long white hair and even longer white beard. He looked like Noah with a weathered and faded blue Red Sox hat on his head. He let go of Lights when he asked him if "ain't that right…?"

"SPACEMAN? You're *The* Spaceman?" I asked awkwardly.

In a voice mixed with California laid back and native New Englander, Spaceman looked at the four of us and said, "you don't look like turkey poachers."

"What's a poacher?" asked Paulie.

"A thief."

"I know what a turkey is, but we haven't seen any turkeys. How would we be stealin' turkeys if we haven't seen any turkeys?" snickered Capisce.

"Whatta you think you've been runnin' after, an ostrich? You boys have been chasing a wild turkey. And, it looks as if you're trespassing on private property—my private property."

"We didn't know it was yours…it was private."

"So that's what that monster, ah, that thing was? A wild turkey?"

"Do you think a forest cuts it's own grass? It looks like Fenway Park, for cryin-out-loud. Gimme a break. You never noticed? And yes, that was a wild turkey, one of my wild turkeys. You boys truly are city kids."

I looked around and felt really embarrassed for all of us. Why hadn't I noticed something was different when I could smell the newly fresh cut grass—and in the middle of the woods? Doesn't everyone have their forest grass cut? I was glad I wasn't the Spaceman's son. Could you imagine having to mow this lawn? I thought. We had to be tented out on two football fields. It must take a week for the poor kid to cut this lawn.

* * *

"Who are you kids, anyway? I don't recognize you from around here."

The guys looked to me for obvious reasons—I was the one who kept emailing The Spaceman. "Spaceman, I'm, we're, the ones who've been emailing you about helping Red Sox pitcher, Lefty Van Weller. You agreed to meet us tomorrow at the Craftsbury Inn and Restaurant. Do you remember? You said you're willing to help the Sox because anything's better than seeing the Yankees win. There's not much time left, either. The season's almost over. How many games left, Lights?"

"Fifty-one, after tonight."

"Fifty-one and they're…"

"Six out."

The radio was on but barely audible through the static. "We're the kids from Belmont?" I asked holding my breath he'd remember.

"Belmont? How'd you kids…ya know, I used to live in Belmont? When I played for the Sox I used to jog into Fenway from my house. I remember it was a quiet town, a small town. But that was many moons ago."

"Knockout!" We glared at each other in disbelief. A real-life baseball star living in *our* town. That had to be the most awesomest knockout happening that, well, that ever happened in Belmont. Even the time old man Pop Weisel drove his car into the donut shop window and everybody had free donuts and cakes has anything *that* knockout happened in Belmont. I wished I had been alive when Spaceman lived in Belmont. I would've rode my bike by his house every day…but I would've never, ever bothered him.

"That the Sox game you're listening to? Can hardly hear it up in these parts. Look, guys, I wouldn't feel right knowing you're out here sleepin.'—and worryin' that maybe the wild turkeys are gobblin' you up."

He shined the flashlight on our faces and started to laugh loud and long—we must've looked like we had seen a ghost.

"You should see your faces. I'm only joking. Boy, you kids are *real* city kids. Look, why don't you gather up your stuff—my place is just through those woods. You can sleep there tonight, be my guest, watch the game—I have a 72-inch plasma television. Whatta you say? Maybe I can see what's ailing Lefty."

The four of us couldn't believe our ears. Maybe the Spaceman was an old guy, now. And maybe he looked like the old Farmer in the Dell. *But he once played baseball for the*

Boston Red Sox! And nothing, nothing in the whole world to an eleven year old is more knockout cooler than that.

"That would be awesome Mr. Spaceman," we all said stuttering over each other.

"Well all right then. Get your stuff together and follow me. What the heck did you kids do to get here, crawl on your bellies? You have more band-aids on yourselves than Carter has pills."

We folded, stuffed, rolled and packed in two minutes. I tried unsuccessfully to hold onto Twotails but she bounded away to the feet of The Spaceman and followed him into and through the woods—a new found friend.

"Well, we sorta jumped on trains…"

"…and off."

"Were chased by snakes…"

"…and trains, *and* train workers."

"We got soaked…"

"…then fried in the sun."

"Got smacked in the…in the…got hit with a fence where it hurt…"

"…then fell in some sticky burr bushes."

"Got attacked by a wild turkey…"

"…and then shot at."

Spaceman stopped and turned to us. "You kids did all that to come see me—to help out the Red Sox? They should build statues and dedicate them to you kids at Fenway Park. That's devotion my new buddies, that's devotion."

You would've had to chisel away the smile that had formed on my face that night. My statue, our statues at Gate A, right next to the statue of Ted Williams. We looked at each other and nodded, all of us grinning like the Cheshire Cat. I bet the guys were thinking the same—how knockout would *my* statue look!

TWENTY-TWO
WORLD SERIES GAME 7
BOSTON RED SOX vs NEW YORK METS

Our parents were kind enough (to be honest we kicked and complained so much they gave up) to let us stay up late on a school night to watch the last game of the very long baseball season—it didn't hurt it was game seven of the World Series. It was, on a long list of cliches, a do or die game, a win or go home, a winner takes all, well, you get the picture. The series between the Boston Red Sox and of all teams, the other hated New York team, the Mets, was tied at three games a piece. The winner of game seven would be the champion—and the four of us wouldn't miss this for all the money in the world.

"I can't take it," complained Capisce.

"I hear ya, *but isn't this knockout?*" yelled Paulie.

"I'm gonna die if they lose," squealed Lights.

"Guys, guys, it's just another game...*yeah, right*!" I yelled as the throw pillows came flying at me. It *was* just another game, if you came from Delaware, Kansas, or the moon. But if you came from Paulie's, Lights's, Capisce's, and my little slice of the world, it was the difference between our dreams being peaceful or filled with horror, our orange juice being sweet or tasting like mud, our shoulders being straight, or stooped. As Lights put it, winning or losing *was* the difference between LIFE and DEATH! And that goes for the whole nation of Red Sox fans.

"Only three days rest…"

"Don't start, Lights. We all know Lefty's going on three days rest."

"I'm just sayin'…"

"'I'm just saying,' we know what you're saying, Mr. Negative. By the way, nice to have you back with us Mr. Positive."

"He's right Capisce," said Paulie. "It's got nothin' to do with being negative. Lefty's never pitched on only three days rest, so who knows how he's gonna feel."

"If he does *exactly* what Spaceman told him then there's no way he'll lose. Has he lost since that day?" I asked.

"Noooo," came their response.

"Give it to us Lights," I asked, never tiring to hear the statistics memorized by our statistician savant.

"He has nine wins and zero losses, with a 1.45 ERA. Should be eleven wins but the bullpen blew a couple of games—but they won those games, too."

"So, exactly why are we worried? The guy's on a knockout streak. Dare I say, the guy's on…"

"FIRE!" They sang on cue.

"Guys, guys, ssshhh. The game's about to start. Where's the picture, where's the picture," I repeated in panic.

"Right where it always is," snorted Capisce. He walked over to the picture of a smiling Spaceman with the four of us, and Twotails, looking shocked, and took it off the wall where it had been hanging for the past two months.

"Pass it around, quick. Ya know we all have to touch it before the first pitch and put it back. Where's Twotails? She's gotta paw it, too."

"I got her. Are we ready?"

And in order we did what had become our new ritual before every Red Sox game—first me, then Lights, then Paulie, then Capisce, and finally Twotails with her perpetually dirty paw, touched the autographed picture of The Spaceman.

"Read it for good luck, would ya Tags?"

"Absolutemente Lights, it would be my pleasure…"

"To my new buddies and eternally devoted Red Sox fans, who should have statues named in their honor—Lights, Paulie, Capisce, Tags, and Twotails—keep the faith and someday your faith will repay you. Your friend, Spaceman."

"Knockout," we all said under our breath as Capisce gently hung the picture back on the wall.

EPILOGUE

Lights tossed a rock against my window (a habit he had gotten in to that if my dad caught him would buy him a boot in the you know what) that woke me from my Saturday morning sleep. I tossed Twotails off my bed when I threw back the covers. "Sorry old girl," I mumbled, rubbing the sleep out of my eyes. Before standing I glared at my Red Sox player posters hanging on my wall—Henry, Wallace, LC, Lozciano, Palagrini, Otto, and Lefty—alongside the baseball schedule. I searched the schedule and found today's date. Lights banging on my window this early on a Saturday morning meant one thing. "Look at that, Twotails." I ran to the window and pushed it up. Finally, I never thought this day would arrive.

Lights was standing in the bushes below my window. "I figured you'd be up and dressed already," Lights said impatiently. "The guys are waiting for you at my house."

"Yeah, sorry. I overslept."

"*Overslept*? How could you have overslept? We've only

been waiting for this day since last year. It's Opening Day, Tags!"

"I know. It's just, well, I've been thinking about this plan, and I guess I just slept late."

"What kind of plan? Ya can tell me I won't tell the guys."

Yeah right, I laughed. "I'll tell ya all when I see you at your house."

"Ah, can you give me a hint?"

"I'm not sure because *I'm* not sure. If that makes any sense. The only thing I can tell you is think The Brain."

"The Brain? Okay, The Brain it is. Two things, Tags. Wear your white Hilberto Otto shirt, and you promised to tell us that story."

"I'll see you in a few minutes." As Lights scampered away my heart soared in anticipation at the beginning chapter of another summer of hope, faith, and trust in the only thing that mattered to us four kids - our favorite baseball team - The Boston Red Sox. Today was *our* beginning - Lights, Paulie, Capisce, and Tags. Our first official "Opening Day," our first free school's out Saturday, and our Opening Day at the park we built at the town dump - the new Fenway Park. Life couldn't get any better. .

The air was still cool these early June mornings, but by afternoon it would bring along the lazy laid-back summer euphoria that only a kid could still eat up and savor without consequences. I smiled at the sky - deep blue for miles and miles with not a cloud in sight. A great day for a doubleheader.

Before I left the open window to get ready, I reminded myself four things; my white number "35" Hilberto Otto jersey, tell the guys the story of Ratso Risoli, work on The

Plan more, and always, always, always, never forget - there IS life after death!